She relaxed against him, for the first time in eight months feeling one hundred percent safe.

Neither said a word, and she was grateful for the silence that revealed more than words.

She was almost asleep when Alex finally stroked a strand of hair away from her face and spoke. "This has been wonderful, but it doesn't solve anything."

With that simple sentence reality slammed back in. Somebody had been at her window. Somebody had given her a note that terrified her with its implication. Was it all just a silly prank or did it imply something more dangerous?

"I guess my next move will be to go see Luke."

"I don't want you going to talk to him alone," Alex said.

She started to protest, but he placed a finger against her lips. "You need somebody on your side, Brittany, and I want to be that man."

D0035588

Dear Reader,

There's something about a man wearing a tool belt low on slim male hips that I find attractive. Maybe it's because the tool belt implies a man who can get a job done, somebody you can depend on to fix whatever is broken.

When sexy Alex Crawford shows up at Brittany Grayson's front door to build a deck on the back of her house, the last thing he's looking for is romance, especially with a woman who had barely escaped being one of the victims of a serial killer.

All he wants is to build a nice life for him and his six-year-old daughter, Emily. But when danger grows near, it will take everything he carries in his tool belt and much more to save the woman he's grown to love and the daughter who owns his heart.

Yes, there's definitely something about a handsome man in a tool belt. I know. I married one years ago and he's still getting the job done and fixing the things that need to be fixed, including my heart.

Happy reading!

Carla Cassidy

* * *

CARLA CASSIDY

Tool Belt Defender

ROMANTIC

SUSPENSE

ISBN-13: 978-0-373-27757-5

TOOL BELT DEFENDER

Books by Carla Cassidy

Harlequin Romantic Suspense

CARLA CASSIDY

is an award-winning author who has written more than one hundred books for Silhouette Books and Harlequin Books. In 1995, she won Best Silhouette Romance from *RT Book Reviews* for *Anything for Danny*. In 1998, she also won a Career Achievement Award for Best Innovative Series from *RT Book Reviews*.

Carla believes the only thing better than curling up with a good book to read is sitting down at the computer with a good story to write. She's looking forward to writing many more books and bringing hours of pleasure to readers.

This book is dedicated to my very own
tool belt defender, Frank.

After all these years you still know exactly what tool
to use to keep me feeling safe and protected and loved.
Thank you and I love you.

Chapter 1

He was a hot hunk in a tight white T-shirt, a pair of worn jeans and a tool belt riding low on his lean hips. He was nothing like what Brittany Grayson had expected.

When she'd called Chad Warren, one of the local carpenters in the small town of Black Rock, Kansas, to see about him building a deck on the back of her house, he'd told her he was already booked for the spring but would send an old college friend of his who had recently moved to town.

Chad was a good old boy, fifty pounds overweight, who believed beer pong should be a nationally recognized sport. It was silly, but she'd just assumed his college buddy would be like him. But the man standing on her front porch didn't look like a peer of Chad's;

rather he looked as if he'd stepped off the slick pages of some hot-hunk calendar.

"Brittany?" His voice was deep and pleasant and made her realize she'd been staring at him open-mouthed through the screen door.

"Yes, I'm Brittany and you must be…" Her mind suddenly went blank.

"Alex. Alex Crawford, Chad's friend. You called him about a deck?"

"Yes, I did." She hesitated before opening the screen door to allow him inside. There had been no men except for her brothers inside her home since she'd moved back in a little over a month ago.

As she unlocked the screen, she realized she wasn't quite ready yet to allow a stranger inside, especially a male stranger. Instead she stepped outside where the late April sun was warm and the air smelled of newly bloomed flowers.

"It's nice to meet you, Alex. Let's walk around back and I'll show you what I have in mind," she said. She frowned as she realized there was no car in her driveway. "Did you walk here?" she asked.

His eyes were a warm blue that stood out against his tanned face and were complemented by his slightly shaggy dark hair. "I live three doors up." He pointed up the street to the Walker home that had been on the market for a while.

"How long have you lived there?"

"I moved in about six weeks ago," he replied as they walked around the side of the house toward the back.

That explained why she didn't know the Walkers

had moved out and Mr. Hardbody had moved in. Six weeks ago she'd still been living at her brother Benjamin's house trying to heal from the trauma she'd lived through.

As they reached the backyard she motioned toward the small broken brick patio that existed just outside the back door. "What I'd like is a wooden deck big enough to hold a barbecue pit and an umbrella table and maybe some plants and, of course, lots and lots of people."

He nodded and pulled a tape measure from his tool belt. "An outdoor entertainment area," he said.

"Exactly," she replied and watched as he began to walk the site. The last thing Brittany had wanted to think about over the past eight months of her life was men. But looking at Alex Crawford definitely gave her a slight flutter of pure feminine pleasure.

When she'd been held captive by a serial killer for four long months, she'd spent her time thinking about all the things she would do if she escaped, if she managed to live.

She hadn't fantasized about love or having babies. She hadn't thought about men or hot sex. Rather she'd thought about a deck where she could invite all her friends and family to share good times with her. And now she was finally going to see those fantasies come to fruition.

"I'd say what you want is about eighteen by twenty-four," Alex said as the tape measure zipped back into its metal case.

"And I'd like a railing around it with an opening to step down into the yard," she said.

He nodded and smiled. "I can do that."

The man had a smile with the capacity to stop time. A wave of warmth washed over Brittany as she tried to stay focused on the matter at hand. "How long will it take?"

He frowned, the gesture doing nothing to detract from his attractiveness. "It will take maybe a week once we get started. I work weekdays from about eight in the morning until about three-thirty and I have a couple of young men who help out, but I don't work on the weekends."

Probably he took the weekends to spend with his family, she thought. A man who looked like Alex Crawford probably had a wife who looked like a supermodel. "So, you'll call me with a bid?"

"If you give me just a few minutes I'll have a bid for you now." He pulled out a small pad and a pencil.

His dark hair shone richly in the overhead sunlight and Brittany suddenly felt the need to get some distance from him. "Why don't I go get us each a glass of lemonade?" she suggested.

He looked up and smiled again and another rivulet of warmth swept through her. "That sounds great."

She escaped back into the house and went through the living room to the kitchen. For a moment she stood at the window and watched him as he once again walked off the area where the deck would be built.

Surely her response to him was nothing more than a healthy awakening of emotions that had been dormant for far too long. She moved away from the window and poured the lemonade into two tall plastic tumblers.

She would be twenty-six in two months—it was only natural that she might appreciate the sight of a good-looking man. She should be glad that normal feelings were finally beginning to return to her.

For the past several months she'd alternated between numbness and an irrational fear as she'd tried to reintegrate back into the life that had been stolen from her for four agonizing months. Nightmares, panic attacks—she'd had them all and had begun to believe she'd never have a normal moment again. It was nice that this normal moment was a healthy dose of lust.

She walked out the back door and motioned him to one of the four chairs at the old table that was on the broken brick patio. "Thanks," he said as he took the drink from her. "I've got some figures for you." He handed her a piece of paper that had his bid written on it. "If you agree, then I'll write up a contract for you to sign."

The figure was about what she'd expected. "Looks good to me." She leaned back in her chair and offered him a tentative smile. "Chad mentioned that the two of you went to college together."

"We did. I went on to law school and got a job in Chicago and Chad came back here."

"From lawyer to carpenter? Quite a leap," she observed. "What brings you back to Black Rock?"

"My wife's family is from here and after several

years of doing the high-powered, high-stress corporate thing, I decided I was ready for a change of pace."

A small laugh escaped Brittany. "The difference in pace between Chicago and Black Rock, Kansas, is like the difference between a pit bull and a stuffed dog." She wasn't surprised that the man was married.

He laughed. "You've got that right, but Black Rock is just what I needed." He tilted his glass up and drained it and then stood. "If you agree with everything I can start work tomorrow, given I can get a lumber delivery."

She got up from her chair and took his empty glass and together they walked around the side of the house to the front.

"Is it your birthday or something?" he asked.

She looked at him in confusion. "No, why?"

He pointed to her mailbox where a bright red balloon was tied and bobbed and danced in the slight warm breeze. Shock ripped through her and the glasses slid from her hands, crashing to the grass at her feet.

It's party time. The nightmarish voice whispered in her brain as memories attacked her. The cell where she'd been kept, the promise of a party when all the cells were filled with helpless women, the final moment when red balloons had danced up to the ceiling of the old shed. *It's party time.*

"Brittany, are you all right?"

Alex's voice pulled her back from the dark abyss she'd nearly fallen into and she tore her gaze from the balloon and looked into his concerned eyes.

"I'm fine," she replied, aware that her voice was shaky and hoping he didn't notice.

"Are you sure?" He bent down and picked up the glasses.

She nodded, even though she wasn't at all sure that she was fine. Thank God the glasses were plastic and hadn't shattered when she'd dropped them. She took them from him, hoping he didn't notice the trembling of her hands. "Silly me. Just a touch of clumsiness. You'll call me and let me know if you're coming tomorrow?"

"I'll head home now and order the necessary lumber and other supplies. If they can deliver tomorrow then I'll give you a call." He eyed her worriedly, but she forced a cheerful smile to her lips.

"Do you need me to write you a check now for the materials?" she asked.

"That's not necessary." His eyes gleamed with a teasing light. "I know where you live."

"Thanks, Alex. Hopefully I'll see you tomorrow." She turned on wooden legs and headed for the house, an urgent need to get inside and lock the door filling her.

She didn't wait to watch him walk down the sidewalk toward his place; rather she turned on her heels and half ran toward her front door. Once inside she slammed it shut and locked it.

Leaning heavily against the solid wood door she told herself she was overreacting, that maybe there was a child's birthday party someplace on the street or a graduation celebration and somebody had just tied the balloon on her mailbox by accident.

Surely there was a logical reason for the balloon. It had nothing to do with the man who had called himself The Professional. He was dead. She'd seen his body after he'd been killed. He was no longer capable of having a "party" complete with red balloons and death.

Still, the legacy he'd left behind sickened her and even though she knew it was totally irrational, that balloon tied to her mailbox made her fear in her heart that somehow The Professional wasn't done with her yet.

As Alex walked back toward his house his head was filled with thoughts of Brittany Grayson. She was something of a celebrity in the small town. Last fall a serial killer had held the town of Black Rock hostage when he'd begun kidnapping women. It had taken all four of Brittany's brothers, who were the law in Black Rock, to figure out that The Professional was actually the town vet, Larry Norwood. They'd managed to rescue the women and Norwood had been killed.

It was discovered that he'd committed the same crime in Kansas City, but unfortunately authorities hadn't been able to catch him before he'd tortured and killed the women he'd held captive there.

Brittany had been the first woman kidnapped and the one who had been held the longest. Still, it wasn't the crime that was uppermost in his mind—it was the woman herself.

Brittany Grayson was stunning and something about her had instantly struck him right in the solar plexus.

Her long dark hair had shone richly in the sunshine and although initially her chocolate-brown eyes had been wary, they'd warmed as she'd talked about the deck she wanted.

The gold, sleeveless blouse she'd worn had emphasized intriguing golden flecks in the very depths of her dark eyes and her jeans had hugged her slender frame and showcased her long legs.

As he approached the two-story house he now called home, he noticed it was time for the first lawn mowing of the season and reminded himself that he wanted to plant flowers in the bed along the porch and down the walkway.

Coming from a high-rise condo in Chicago where there had been no outside maintenance or yard work for him to be responsible for, moving into this house had been daunting but would definitely be worth it in the long run.

As he opened the door he heard the sound of little feet running and before he could prepare himself completely six-year-old Emily launched herself into his arms.

"Daddy!" She placed her hands on both of his cheeks, making it impossible for him to look at anything but her, which of course he didn't mind. The pint-size blonde with her bright green eyes and long pigtails was the most important thing in Alex's life.

"What?" he asked as he carried her into the living room and then leaned down to place her on the floor.

"Grandma said I've been so good while you've been gone, I should get ice cream after dinner tonight."

"She did, did she?"

"Guilty as charged," Rose Tyler said as she walked into the living room.

Alex smiled warmly at the older woman. She was an attractive woman, her short gray hair perfectly coiffed, clad in a pair of navy slacks and a tailored white-and-navy blouse.

She had certainly been instrumental in Alex's decision to move to Black Rock. When his wife, Linda, had died eighteen months ago, Alex had tried to be a good and present single parent, but with his work schedule as a lawyer in a big firm Emily had spent more time with babysitters than with him.

It had been an unacceptable reality for a little girl reeling from her mother's death. Here in Black Rock not only did Alex have a new occupation that he found far more rewarding than what he'd been doing and allowed him more time with his daughter, but Emily also had a loving grandmother who only lived a block away from their house and was available to babysit day or night.

"Then I guess ice cream it is," he agreed and laughed as Emily clapped her hands together and then did a little dance to show her pleasure. "I have to go tell Lady Bear. She'll be so happy." She dashed from the room and up the stairs toward her bedroom.

"You've done such a good job with her, Alex," Rose

said with a smile. "And I'll never be able to thank you enough for moving here so I can be a part of her life." Her smile wavered slightly and she placed a slender, wrinkled hand over her heart. "When we lost Linda I was afraid that I'd lose you and Emily, too."

"Don't kid yourself, this move was as much for me as it was about you and Emily," he replied. "I was more than ready for a change of lifestyle and I think this is going to be a great place to raise Emily."

"Did you get the job?" Rose asked as she pulled on the white cardigan sweater she'd brought with her when she'd arrived to watch Emily.

"I did. If all goes well, starting tomorrow morning I'll be working on a deck at Brittany Grayson's house."

Rose frowned. "That poor girl. I can't imagine her having the courage to move back to her house all alone after what she's been through. She'd got to be one of the strongest people I know."

"She definitely seems ready to move on with her life," he replied.

"Speaking of moving on, I'd better get out of here," Rose said, as she picked up her purse from the sofa.

Alex walked to the bottom of the staircase. "Emily, Grandma is leaving. Come down and tell her goodbye."

Emily came down the stairs, her favorite pink stuffed bear in her arms. "Lady Bear wanted to say goodbye, too."

"By all means, I wanted to say goodbye to Lady Bear," Rose replied as she shook the bear's pink paw.

Alex watched the goodbyes exchanged between

Rose and Emily and Lady Bear and tried not to worry that Emily's attachment to the stuffed animal bordered on obsessive.

The bear had been a gift from a friend attending Linda's funeral and Alex had a feeling that all of Emily's love for her mother had been transferred to the stuffed animal.

"Are you sure you don't want me to drive you home?" Alex asked Rose when the goodbyes were finished and Emily had gone back upstairs to her room.

"No, thank you. A little exercise is good for me, and besides, it's only a block. You'll call me later and let me know what the schedule is for tomorrow?"

"Yeah, but I should be able to work it so that I'm home when Emily gets off the school bus," he replied. "If something changes I'll let you know."

A few minutes later he stepped out onto the porch and watched as Rose walked up the sidewalk. Rose had lost her husband in a car accident five years ago and then had lost her only child, Linda. There was nobody Alex admired more in the world than his mother-in-law, who, despite the tragedies she'd suffered, continued to not only put one foot in front of the other but seemed to seek out happiness whenever and wherever she could find it.

She'd been by Alex's side when Linda had died, and he knew the anger she'd felt toward her daughter, an anger that still burned inside Alex when the grief wasn't filling him up. But Rose had hidden her anger well as she'd tended to her daughter in Linda's last days.

When Rose disappeared from his sight he turned and went back into the house. As he climbed the stairs to Emily's room, he checked his wristwatch. It was only a little after four.

He found Emily sitting at the child-size table and chairs in her room. Lady Bear sat in the chair opposite her and there was a coloring book open not only in front of Emily, but also in front of the bear.

"Hi, Daddy. We decided to color you a picture," she said as Alex folded his long legs and sat in the little chair next to hers.

"You know how much I love your pictures," he replied. In fact, the front of his refrigerator was laden with Emily's artwork. He watched for a few minutes as she colored a blue sky and a pink house. When she started in on the yellow sun he spoke.

"You know, I was thinking, maybe since you were such a good girl for grandma while I was gone, we might have ice cream before dinner."

Emily's green eyes opened wide and the yellow crayon rolled out of her small hand and across the table. "Before dinner? Like right now?"

"Like right now," he replied. He laughed as Emily was out of her chair with Lady Bear in her arms before he could blink his eyes.

"Now, that's a good plan," she exclaimed.

"But only one scoop. I don't want to completely ruin your appetite for dinner."

"Okay, maybe one scoop before dinner and one scoop after," Emily replied, making Alex laugh.

Ten minutes later they were headed down the sidewalk to Main Street where Izzy's Ice Cream Parlor had quickly become their favorite shop in town. He'd managed to convince her that Lady Bear didn't need to come with them, that she'd much prefer some pretend honey when they got home than an ice cream cone now. As they walked Emily regaled him with stories about her day in school.

Thankfully, Emily had adjusted well to changing schools, loved her teacher and had already made new friends. She also loved having a backyard and had begun making noises about getting a dog. So far she'd adjusted to the move far better than Alex.

Although he'd been ready for the change, looked forward to a new occupation, a new lifestyle, he hadn't expected the loneliness.

In Chicago there had been business dinners, fund-raisers and late nights at the office to keep the loneliness at bay. Here most evenings existed of a bottle of beer and the sound of crickets from outside the window. He definitely hadn't expected this kind of aching loneliness.

But he didn't intend to ever marry again, and was reluctant to even date. The last thing he wanted to do was invite a string of women into Emily's life, women who would never be more than temporary.

As they walked by Brittany Grayson's house his thoughts returned to her. According to the local gossip she'd been strong and courageous during her captivity, and the other women who had been held captive had given her credit for keeping them sane.

If he did ever decide to marry again, which he seriously doubted he would, he would choose a strong woman. He'd loved Linda, but it hadn't taken him long into the marriage to realize she was childlike in her fears of life and that fear was ultimately what had led to her death.

Still, even though he told himself he had no desire to get involved with any woman right now, he couldn't help the anticipation that swept through him as he thought of seeing Brittany again.

He couldn't help but wonder if she was the fearless heroine everyone called her or just a damaged victim of a heinous crime.

Chapter 2

"Maybe you moved back here too soon," Brittany's eldest brother, Tom, said to her the next morning. He'd stopped by on his way into work as sheriff of Black Rock. He was a handsome man in his khaki uniform, but he had that stern big-brother look on his face that drove Brittany crazy.

"I mean, if the sight of a balloon threw you for a loop, then maybe you weren't ready to be out on your own," he added.

"It was time for me to get out of Benjamin and Edie's place. They're newlyweds and need their own space and it was time for me to get on with my life." Brittany got up from the table to refill her coffee mug. "Besides, it didn't throw me for a loop. I just wondered who had tied it to my mailbox and why." She topped off her coffee and then rejoined him at the table. "It was just natural curiosity."

Tom smiled at her knowingly. "Most people's voices don't quiver when expressing their feelings of natural curiosity."

"I'm sorry I even mentioned it," she retorted ruefully.

"You know you could always stay with us if you aren't ready to be out on your own. Peyton wouldn't mind having you with us."

Love for her brother surged up inside Brittany. He and his wife were newlyweds, as well, and had Peyton's little daughter, Lilly, to dote on. Besides, Brittany didn't want to live with any of her brothers anymore. She wanted...needed to be out on her own.

"Thanks, but I'm fine here. In fact I'm having a new deck built."

"Chad doing it?" he asked.

Brittany shook her head. "He was busy so he recommended a friend of his, Alex Crawford."

Tom frowned. "I don't think I've met him."

"He's only been in town about six weeks. He moved into the Walker house."

He nodded. "Have you given any thought to coming back to work?" he asked.

Before her kidnapping Brittany had also been a member of the Black Rock law-enforcement team. She'd worked beneath Tom as a deputy along with her other brothers Benjamin and Caleb. Her brother Jacob had worked for the FBI in Kansas City, but during the time Brittany had been kidnapped he had returned to Black Rock and was now also a deputy for the town.

"I'm not ready yet," she replied. "I hate to leave you shorthanded but to be perfectly honest, I'm not sure I want to return." The words formed a lump in the back of her throat.

Tom lifted an eyebrow in surprise. He leaned back in his chair, his eyes studying her. "You don't have to come back if it doesn't feel right, and don't worry about leaving me shorthanded."

"But isn't Benjamin leaving in a week or so?"

"Two weeks."

Brittany's brother Benjamin had for years divided his energies between the jobs of working as a deputy and ranching on the family homestead. He'd finally decided to ranch full-time and was quitting his duties as deputy.

"Have you given any thought to what you'd rather do if you don't come back?" Tom asked.

"Not really. I thought I'd take some online college classes and keep my options open."

"What about money? Are you okay?"

Brittany smiled. "I'm fine. I had some savings and I'm using some of my inheritance for the deck."

"I figured you'd already spent all that money on shoes and purses," Tom said teasingly and then checked his watch. "I've got to get out of here. If I don't check in soon, Caleb will be sitting in my chair with his feet up on my desk." He downed the last of his coffee and then got up from the table and carried his cup to the sink.

Brittany walked him to her front door where he turned and touched her lightly on the tip of her nose. "You'll be okay. Go shopping, buy yourself something completely frivolous. That's always made you feel better in the past."

She watched him as he walked toward the path to his patrol car parked at the curb. She knew he meant well. All of her brothers did, but they all interacted with her as if she were the same person she'd been before the kidnapping, and she wasn't.

She closed the door and locked it, then returned to the kitchen and grabbed her coffee cup. She walked to the back window and stared out at the patio.

A little over eight months ago, before she'd been taken captive, she'd been a spoiled, indulged princess. She'd loved hanging out with her friends at Harley's Bar, a rough-and-tumble tavern that boasted live music on the weekends. She'd loved shopping and lunch out and dating men that weren't necessarily husband material.

She'd often been late to work, knowing that her brothers would cover for her, and living each moment without thought for the next had been her specialty.

She wasn't that woman anymore, but her brothers had failed to see that although her life had been spared, the immature, irresponsible girl she'd been had been killed, leaving her floundering to discover exactly who she was now.

She rubbed her eyes, feeling the grit of exhaustion. The balloon had been gone when she'd gotten up that morning, but the sight of it had kept her awake far too long the night before. She hadn't been able to shake a sense of foreboding that in the light of day seemed rather silly.

She jumped as her phone rang. She didn't recognize the number, but picked it up and answered.

"Brittany, it's Alex."

His deep voice washed over her with a welcome heat and she reminded herself that he was a married man. "Hi, what's up?"

"I thought I'd let you know that the supplies should be delivered around noon today and if you don't mind I'd like to be there when they drop them off."

"No problem. I just can't wait for the project to be done."

"Then I'll see you just before noon."

She hung up and smiled ruefully. It was just her luck that after everything she'd been through the first man who sparked any kind of interest in her was totally off-limits.

Reminding herself that the last thing she needed at this moment in her life was a man, she set about making herself breakfast.

It was about midday when she looked out her back window and saw Alex seated in one of the chairs on her patio. She opened the back door and stepped outside.

"You should have told me you were here," she said as he smiled at her and stood.

"I didn't want to bother you. They told me the delivery would be around noon, but that usually means anywhere between noon and four."

She waved him back down and sank into the chair opposite his and tried not to notice that he looked just as handsome today as he had the day before. "Would you like something to drink?" she asked.

"No, thanks. I'm good."

He was better than good, she thought. "It's a gorgeous day to start the project," she said.

He smiled. "Nothing better than a perfect spring day for a little work outside."

"Have you had a chance to explore Black Rock?" She just wanted to make conversation, to have a reason to remain sitting across from him and enjoy the view.

"We've definitely discovered Izzy's Ice Cream Parlor. I think it's going to be our favorite hangout until winter comes."

"When winter does arrive then you'll have to go out to Mathew's pond on the north side of town. If the temperature is right he sets up fire barrels around the edge of the pond and half the town shows up there on the weekends to ice-skate."

"Sounds like fun."

"How's your wife coping with small-town life?" she asked, needing to remind herself that that he was a married man and then maybe that thousand-watt smile of his wouldn't have so much power over her.

"Actually, I lost my wife almost two years ago. Being a single parent was part of my reason for changing careers and deciding to move here. My wife's mother lives here and I thought my daughter could use the support of a loving grandmother."

"I'm so sorry," Brittany said, knowing the simple

words weren't adequate for the depth of loss he'd suffered. Her heart went out to him. He had not only lost the woman he loved, but apparently had made the choice to leave his career behind and move because in his mind it was the best thing he could do for his daughter.

Someplace in the back of her mind she realized this meant that Alex was a single man. Not that it mattered to her. No matter how hot he was, she just wasn't ready for a man in her life.

All she wanted from Alex was a deck where she could have her friends and family over for barbecues and good times. Beyond that she knew what she needed most was time to heal, and that was something she had to do all alone.

"It's all right," he replied. "Time passes and life goes on. My main goal is just to make sure that Emily is okay. Emily is my six-year-old daughter."

Now she understood why he didn't work weekends and worked relatively short days. "You mentioned that your wife's mother lives here. Would I have known your wife?"

He shook his head. "Linda never lived here in Black Rock. Her parents, Rose and Harry, moved here after Linda and I got married."

"Rose Tyler," Brittany said.

"That's right."

Brittany smiled. "She's a nice lady. She does a lot of charity work here in town."

"She's the greatest," he agreed. "And best of all

she's a babysitter who never complains about long hours."

"What about your parents?" she asked.

"They live a wonderful life in Italy. They weren't exactly what you'd call doting parents and so I knew not to turn to them when Linda died."

At that moment the conversation was cut short as the truck from the lumberyard arrived. Brittany stood to the side and watched as it was unloaded. The truth of the matter was she watched Alex as he helped Ed Burton from the lumberyard unload. She watched in fascination as his T-shirt stretched taut across his back with each load he lifted.

She'd found the tidbit of information about his parents intriguing but told herself she didn't want to know more intimate details of his life.

Even if she were ready for a man in her life and even though she found Alex incredibly sexy, she still wouldn't want to have any relationship with him.

Brittany wasn't sure she wanted children of her own. There was no way she'd want to take on somebody else's. She still needed to work on herself and wouldn't have the time or energy to deal with a grieving child.

No, she would be happy to admire Alex's taut body over the next couple of days but there wouldn't be anything more between them, not that he'd made any sign that he was even remotely interested in her.

Within twenty minutes everything was off the truck and stacked neatly on one side of the yard and Ed Burton drove away. Brittany was surprised when

Buck Harmon and another young man appeared in the backyard.

"There you are," Alex said with a smile to the two young men.

"Sorry we're late. Gary had to stuff his face with a sandwich before we left his house," Buck said. He raised a hand to Brittany in greeting.

"These are my helpers," Alex said. "I'm assuming you know Buck and Gary."

"I know Buck," she replied. And what she knew of him she didn't like. At twenty-four years old Buck had a reputation for trouble. He worked odd jobs, drank more than he should and could be a hothead. More than once as a deputy she'd had to give him a stern warning about some infraction or another. "But I don't believe I've met Gary before," she added.

"Gary Cox." He strode over to her and held out his hand. The freckles on his face danced as he offered her a friendly smile and shook her hand with an adult firmness. His coppery hair gleamed in the sunlight as he stepped back from her. "I'm Buck's friend and I've been helping Alex on some of his jobs."

He looked like an odd companion for Buck. Gary gave the impression of being a puppy dog, eager to please and slightly goofy. "Nice to meet you, Gary," she said.

"Now that the introductions are out of the way, it's time to get to work," Alex said.

"And I'll just get out of your way," Brittany replied. She went back inside the house but stood at the back window and watched as Alex and the younger men got to work.

She wondered if Alex knew that Buck wasn't the most trustworthy person in town. Buck had had more than his share of run-ins with all of the Graysons. If she got a chance she'd mention her concerns about him to Alex, but in the meantime she watched as the work began on the dream that had helped keep her sane through her months of captivity.

Watching Alex work should become a national pastime, she thought as she watched him pick up a hole digger and hand it to Buck.

She turned away, deciding she needed to stop watching Alex and find something more constructive to do. She'd been meaning to clean out her closet since moving back into the house. She'd lost about fifteen pounds while being held by The Professional and intended to donate a lot of the clothes that were now too big for her to charity.

She kept her mind blank as she worked, knowing that if she gave it free rein it always went back to the filthy cell where she'd been held, counting the days, the very minutes to death.

It was just after three when she heard a knock on her back door and hurried to answer. Once again a rivulet of warmth wiggled through her as she saw Alex.

"We're knocking off for the day," he said when she opened the door. "We've got the posts up but they need to set. Since tomorrow is Saturday we'll give them the weekend and we'll be here bright and early on Monday morning."

"Sounds good," she replied. "Then I'll see you on Monday."

"Have a good weekend," he said and then he was gone.

She hadn't realized how much the sound of the male voices coming from the backyard throughout the afternoon had comforted her.

Now she found the silence slightly oppressive. She moved the box of oversize clothing she'd packed next to the front door and then called a local charity for a pickup the next day.

Sitting down on the sofa, she punched the remote control to turn on the television, just wanting the noise to fill the emptiness of the otherwise silent house.

For almost three months she'd been alone in the shed, with only the sound of The Professional's voice to occasionally break the silence with his taunts and threats. She'd discovered that now she didn't do silence well.

Her thoughts instantly drifted back to Alex. There was no question that she felt a visceral physical pull toward him. And why shouldn't she? He was definitely attractive and she was definitely lonely.

She only left the house for grocery shopping and then only when it was absolutely necessary. She told herself it wasn't fear that kept her inside but rather the stares and whispers that followed her anywhere she went.

A couple of the friends she'd had before being kidnapped had contacted her after her rescue, but she'd realized they seemed more interested in finding out the grisly details of the crime than her well-being.

Although she was happy that her brothers had all found love while she'd been gone, the fact that they were now building lives with loved ones and had a place where they belonged only made her loneliness deeper. She didn't know where she belonged anymore.

The late afternoon and evening crept by. She fixed herself a salad for dinner, then watched some more TV. Finally at nine o'clock she went into her bedroom and got ready for bed.

She'd just turned out the light and closed her eyes when her phone rang. Fumbling on the nightstand, she turned on the lamp next to the bed and looked at the caller ID on the phone.

Anonymous caller.

She frowned and sat up. Probably a sales call or some stupid survey, she thought as she grabbed the receiver.

"Hello?"

Nobody replied, although she knew somebody was on the other end. She could hear the soft sound of breathing. "Hello?" she repeated, this time more firmly. "Who is this?"

Still nobody answered, but the breathing grew louder and she was suddenly cast back in time, back to when The Professional would breathe a little harder, a little faster as he talked about the party of death he intended.

Trapped in a moment of sheer terror, her heart beat frantically and she couldn't catch her breath. Frozen with fear she heard nothing but the sound of the caller breathing…and waiting.

She finally managed to crash the receiver back into the cradle.

She drew several deep breaths and then released a shaky laugh. The Professional was dead. She was safe and a prank phone call had nothing to do with the man who had once planned her death.

The phone call, along with the balloon, had been nothing more than coincidences that had triggered bad memories. There was absolutely no reason for her to be afraid, yet she couldn't stop shaking and she couldn't quiet the dreadful sense of foreboding that slithered through her.

It took a very long time for her heart to finally return to a normal rhythm and even longer before she was ready to turn out the light.

Alex spent much of Saturday working in the yard with Emily. He cut the grass while she raked and bagged the clippings and then they went to the local nursery and picked out flowers to plant along the walk leading from the street to the house.

As they worked Emily kept up a string of chatter, asking him if there were flowers in Heaven, what kinds of flowers they were planting and anything else that entered her brilliant little mind.

It was after dinner and cleanup that he announced he thought a trip to Izzy's was in order to reward them for all their hard work during the day.

At just after seven they left the house and headed

down the sidewalk toward Main Street. It was a beautiful spring evening, unusually warm and with the scent of newly bloomed flowers hanging in the air.

Emily alternated between hopping and skipping next to him. She was a child that rarely just walked. She oozed energy and an exuberant happiness that filled Alex's soul. In the weeks immediately following Linda's death he'd feared that his daughter would never know real happiness again, but she was a testimony to the resilience of the human spirit.

"I'm thinking strawberry," she said thoughtfully as she jumped over a crack in the sidewalk.

"Really?" he replied with amusement. They had this conversation each time they walked to Izzy's. She professed to be thinking about eating some flavor of ice cream but always opted for chocolate ice cream with sprinkles when they got there.

"What are you thinking, Daddy?" she asked.

This was also part of the tradition that had been established in their walks to Izzy's. Alex frowned in mock thoughtfulness. "I'm thinking maybe worm-flavored ice cream."

He was rewarded by her infectious giggles. "Daddy, that's so gross," she exclaimed.

As they walked in front of Brittany's house he was surprised to see her sitting on her porch. "Wait up, Emily," he said. He jogged up the walk to her porch. "Good evening, Ms. Grayson."

"Good evening to you, Mr. Crawford."

Her smile warmed him as Emily came running to

join him. "Emily, this is Ms. Grayson," he said. "My daughter, Emily."

"Hi, Emily. You can call me Brittany," she replied.

"We're going to get ice cream at Izzy's. Want to come with us?" Emily asked.

"Oh, I don't think so. I don't go into town much," Brittany replied, but Alex thought he saw a touch of wistfulness momentarily flit across her beautiful dark eyes.

"Emily, why don't you show Brittany how you can do a cartwheel in the grass?" Alex said.

Emily's face lit up. There was nothing she loved more than showing off her gymnastic skills. "Okay." As she raced off the porch Alex turned back to Brittany.

"And why don't you go into town much?" he asked.

"Watch this, Brittany," Emily yelled from the yard.

She focused her attention on Emily. "You've probably heard about what happened to me."

"I've heard a little bit about it," he admitted.

"That's super, Emily," she called out as Emily performed two perfectly executed cartwheels. "People stare and whisper," she said softly. "It makes me uncomfortable so I just don't go out much."

He heard a hint of loneliness in her voice and it called to his own loneliness. "We're not going to traipse down Main Street in a parade. We're just going to Izzy's for some ice cream."

"This time I'm going to do four cartwheels in a row," Emily yelled.

"Tell you what," Alex continued. "If you feel somebody staring at you and you get all uncomfortable, I'll stick an ice cream cone on my nose and cover my head with sprinkles. Trust me, nobody will be staring at you after that."

She looked at him in surprise and then laughed. By that time Emily had rejoined them. "Did you see me do four cartwheels?"

"I did," Brittany replied. "That was so totally awesome."

"So are you joining us?" Alex asked, vaguely surprised at how much he wanted her to come with them.

She hesitated a long moment and then nodded. "Okay, just let me grab my purse."

"She's pretty," Emily said as Brittany disappeared through her front door.

"Yes, she is," Alex agreed.

"Do you like her?" Emily slid him a sly glance.

"I'm building a deck on the back of her house so she's kind of like my boss right now." The last thing he wanted was for Emily to get any ideas about a budding relationship between him and Brittany.

Since they'd moved to Black Rock Emily had learned about stepmoms and had decided it would be nice to have one. Alex had explained to his daughter that finding a perfect stepmother was more difficult than it seemed and that she shouldn't count on it ever happening.

Brittany stepped back out the front door with her purse slung over her shoulder. "All set."

The two of them fell into step on the sidewalk while

Emily danced just ahead of them. "What kind of ice cream do you like, Brittany?" she asked.

"I'm definitely a chocolate lover," Brittany replied.

"Me, too!" Emily exclaimed. "Daddy says he's going to get worm-flavored ice cream today."

"That's gross," Brittany replied.

Once again Emily laughed in delight. "That's what I told him." She fell into step next to Brittany and gazed up at her. "Since you're daddy's boss, maybe you could tell him that he should let me get two scoops of ice cream instead of just one."

Brittany laughed again and Alex thought he could listen to her laugh for a long time. He was also aware of the scent of her, a clean, fresh floral with a touch of jasmine that teased his senses.

"Let's see when we get there how much arm-twisting we need to do to get your daddy to agree to two scoops," she said.

Emily nodded and then once again danced ahead of them along the sidewalk. "She's a doll," Brittany said.

"She's far too smart for her own good, as stubborn as the day is long, but best of all she's my heart," he replied.

"That's nice. Every little girl needs a father in her life."

"Are your parents here in town?" he asked.

She shook her head, her rich dark hair gleaming in the sunshine. "My parents died a long time ago, but I have four brothers who stepped into the role of father figure and sometimes that feels like four too many," she said ruefully.

He grinned. "One of them is the sheriff, right?"

"Yes, that's Tom. Then there's Jacob, Benjamin and Caleb. Right now they all work as deputies, but Benjamin is quitting in a couple of weeks to ranch full-time."

"And from what I've heard you were also a deputy at one time."

"Before the incident." Her voice held a slight edge of stress. *The incident*—such pitiful words to use to describe what she'd gone through.

"It's been a beautiful day, hasn't it?" He quickly changed the subject. The last thing he wanted to do was ruin this time with her by discussing something she didn't want to talk about. "Emily and I spent the afternoon planting flowers along the walkway to our front door."

"We got flowers with a name like what my daddy sometimes calls me," Emily quipped. "Impatients."

Brittany laughed again and Alex could tell she was relaxing with each minute that passed. There was something tragic about a woman who had lived through what she had and wound up being afraid to leave her own house because of the whispers and stares of the other people in town.

"Once you have my deck up I intend to plant flowers everywhere in the backyard," she said. "I want that deck to be the prettiest place on the planet."

"Then I'll have to make sure that I'm on top of my game and give you a deck that will be the envy of everyone in town," he replied.

By that time they'd reached Izzy's. The ice-cream

parlor was a small shop with half a dozen small round peppermint-pink tables inside and a long refrigerated counter displaying almost every flavor of ice cream imaginable. Much to Alex's mock dismay and Emily's giggles, they had no worm-flavored.

They were the only customers inside, and once they'd ordered and been served the three of them sat at a table near the window where the last of the day's sun was visible, slowly sinking lower onto the horizon.

The conversation centered on the merits of ice cream and the variety of flavors available. Brittany was good with Emily, talking to her with an easiness and respect that Emily responded to in the same way.

There was no question that he was drawn to Brittany. Her thick, shiny hair begged him to tangle his hands in it, her plump lips seemed to ask for a kiss and that scent of her half dizzied him with a simmering desire to seek its source.

He didn't know if his reaction to her was just a manifestation of his loneliness. Or maybe he was drawn to her because she seemed so different from his wife. A core of inner strength shone from Brittany's eyes, a strength he found vastly appealing.

"This was nice," Brittany said as they left Izzy's and began the short walk home. Twilight had fallen and night shadows were beginning to creep in.

"I'm glad you came with us," he replied.

"Me, too," Emily added. "I think you should come with us every time we go to get ice cream."

Brittany smiled at her. "That's just because you got two scoops with me along."

Emily giggled and then sobered a bit. "But I also like you because you're really pretty and you make my dad smile really big."

Alex felt his cheeks warm and tried to find something to say, but Emily wasn't finished yet. "Did you know my mommy is in Heaven?" she asked Brittany.

"Yes, your daddy told me that," Brittany replied.

"Do you think there's ice cream in Heaven?"

Alex saw a whisper of compassion in Brittany's eyes at Emily's question. She stopped walking and crouched down to Emily's level.

"I'd like to think there's ice cream in Heaven. You know, my mommy died, too. Maybe your mommy and mine are having ice cream together right now."

"That would be good," Emily replied with a little smile. "Now, watch how I can jump the cracks in the sidewalk really fast." She raced ahead of them, her pigtails dancing.

"That was nice," he said to Brittany.

She nodded. "It must be tough to be a single dad."

"Emily makes it relatively easy. She's a good kid. Would you like to have dinner with me tomorrow night? I cook a mean steak."

He wasn't sure who was more surprised by the invitation, Brittany or himself. The words had just tumbled out of his mouth as if with a life of their own.

"Thank you, but I always have Sunday dinner with my brothers and their families," she replied.

"Then what about Monday evening?" They stopped in front of her house.

Her brown eyes studied him thoughtfully. "Alex, I'm not looking for any kind of romance."

"I'm not, either," he quickly replied. "I have no intentions of ever marrying again. But I'm new in town and to be honest, I've been a bit lonely. I just thought it would be nice to have a friend to share a meal or spend some time with."

"Okay," she agreed. "As long as we both understand where we're coming from, I'd love to have dinner with you on Monday."

"Great! Why don't we say around six-thirty?"

"Sounds good and thanks for the ice cream." She looked down the walk to Emily. "Bye, Emily," she called.

"Bye, Brittany." Emily waved. "See ya later."

Brittany looked back at Alex. "And I'll see you Monday morning, right?"

"Bright and early," he replied. They said their goodbyes and he watched as she climbed the stairs to her porch and then disappeared into her house.

Emily fell into step beside him and began chatting about her plans to play with the neighbor girl the next day. Alex listened absently and wondered why he wanted to kiss a woman he'd just told he only wanted to be her friend.

Chapter 3

She shouldn't have agreed to dinner. Brittany walked into her kitchen, dropped her purse on the counter and then sank down into one of the kitchen chairs.

Alex Crawford disturbed her in a distinctly pleasant way. Something about him made her heart flutter in her chest and caused her palms to dampen. She liked the way he looked, the way he smelled. She liked the sound of his laughter, so rich and deep, and she liked the way he interacted with his daughter.

As she'd watched him eat his ice cream she'd found herself wondering what his lips would taste like, how his arms would feel wrapped around her.

Dangerous thoughts.

She knew she wasn't ready for a romantic relationship, and as cute and sweet as Emily had been,

Brittany definitely wasn't ready to be a mom. Her brothers would laugh at the very idea and remind her how flighty and immature she was.

Still, she could use a friend and apparently that was what Alex was looking for, too. He was new to town and obviously hadn't made any real friends, and hers had all pretty much deserted her in the months following her rescue while she'd been living with Benjamin and Edie on the family ranch just outside of town.

"Two less lonely people in the world." The words to an old Air Supply song filled her head. Maybe Alex was supposed to be her transitional man, the one who, through his easy friendship, could bridge her way from recovering crime victim to healthy young woman ready for love.

Dinner at Alex's place was nothing to be concerned about, she told herself. Emily would be there, and besides, Brittany had made it clear to Alex she wasn't ready for romance.

She was about to get out of the chair when a shadow darted across the kitchen window. Every muscle in her body froze—except her heart, which roared to a painful gallop.

Somebody was in her yard…just outside of her window. What was he doing out there? Had the person been watching her? Why? The inertia left her and with her heart still beating far too fast, she got up from the table.

Her feet felt leaden with fear as she tentatively approached the window and cautiously peered outside.

Nothing.

Although the evening shadows had thickened, there was still enough ambient light to let her know that there was nobody lurking in her backyard.

Had the shadow just been a figment of her imagination? Had a cloud danced over the moon to create what she'd thought was somebody just outside the house?

She drew a deep breath and backed away from the window, her heart not yet finding its normal rhythm. She felt foolish and yet couldn't halt the feeling of threat that combined with a deep sense of dread that washed over her.

She wished she had her gun, but she'd turned it in to Tom just after she'd been rescued, knowing it would be some time before she was ready, if ever, to go back to work as his deputy.

The fear kept her awake until near dawn when she fell into a restless sleep. She didn't get out of bed until almost noon the next day and as always the sunshine made her fears of the night before seem silly.

She hated the fear, was ashamed of it. It was part of the reason she knew she wasn't ready to go back to her job. A good deputy didn't feel fear. A good deputy didn't think the way she'd thought when she'd been held by a madman.

It was just before six in the evening when she left her house to drive to the family ranch on the edge of town. Since the crime that had taken her away for four months, it had become a tradition that on Sunday the whole family got together at the old homestead for dinner.

As she parked in front of the large, rambling ranch

house, she tried to slough off the exhaustion that had been with her all day long. Two nights of too little sleep had definitely taken its toll.

She was the last to arrive and when she walked through the front door the chaos of family greeted her. Her brothers were all in the great room, Tom's wife Peyton's little girl, Lilly, tottering back and forth between them with squeals of delight.

"Hey, girl." Caleb got out of his chair and greeted her with a kiss on her temple. He stepped back from her and frowned. "What's up with you? You don't look so hot."

She punched him in the arm. "Thanks, you're terrific for a girl's ego." She worried a hand through her long hair. "I'm just tired, that's all. I didn't sleep very well last night."

"Bad night?" Benjamin asked, his dark eyes filled with compassion.

She shrugged. "I thought I saw somebody outside my window. It freaked me out a little bit and I had trouble getting to sleep." She watched as they all exchanged glances.

"You know, Brittany, maybe you should talk to somebody," Jacob said. "You won't talk to us about what happened for those four months. Maybe you need a little therapy."

"I don't need therapy," she replied with a touch of irritation. "I just need a good night's sleep, that's all." She left the great room and her brothers and went into the kitchen where the wives were all gathered.

Of all the women who had become sisters-in-law,

Brittany felt the closest to Layla, Jacob's wife. Layla had been the last victim kidnapped and placed in a cell to await The Professional's final party of death. Although she'd only been captive for a few hours before they had all been rescued, Brittany knew that Layla understood at least part of the kind of terror that Brittany had tasted, had endured throughout her ordeal.

"Mmm, something smells good," she said as she entered the large, cheerful kitchen.

"Roast and potatoes, green beans and hot rolls," Edie, Benjamin's wife, replied. "And Portia brought pies."

Portia, Caleb's wife, patted her five-months-pregnant belly. "I've been dreaming about peach pies for the past week. I keep telling Caleb it must be some sort of strange pregnancy craving."

"I wish I could blame pregnancy hormones for my dreams of chocolate fountains, doughnuts and candy bars. God, I've become such a sugar addict," Layla exclaimed. Brittany laughed and sat on the stool next to her at the kitchen island. "How are you doing? You look tired," Layla said.

"I am," Brittany admitted. "But on a positive note I've started work on the deck I've been talking about forever."

"That's great. Who's doing the work?" Peyton asked.

"A new guy in town. His name is Alex Crawford." Even saying his name created a pleasant pool of warmth in the pit of her stomach.

Layla released a wolf whistle. "I sold him the house. That man is pure sin walking. What? I'm married, not dead," she exclaimed as the others looked at her. "I'm still allowed to look and admire."

"He is easy on the eyes," Brittany admitted, but she didn't mention that she'd agreed to have dinner with him. There was no point when she had no intention of it being anything but a pleasant dinner between friends. Still, she couldn't stop the small shiver of delight that worked through her as she thought about spending more time with him.

Dinner was a wild, chaotic affair with everyone talking over each other and plenty of laughter served all around. Brittany found herself once again counting her blessings that she had such a strong support system in her family.

Still, there was no question that when she saw the small smiles and secretive looks that flew from husband to wife, the touches that spoke of a deeper, lasting intimacy, a wistful ache filled her up inside.

Eventually she wanted what her brothers had found, a love that made a couple into something more, a commitment that was meant to last a lifetime. Even though she yearned for that, she didn't think she was ready for it at this time in her life.

She still jumped at shadows, trembled when nobody talked on the phone. She didn't particularly like the dark and knew it was going to take time for her to finally be one-hundred-percent healthy.

"Just think, within a couple of weeks I'll be able to have you all over for a barbecue on my new deck," Brittany said as the meal was winding down.

"I like my burger medium well and my beer ice-cold," Jacob said. He shot a glance to Layla. "And my woman silent and naked."

Layla snorted. "I have no problem with the naked part, but you know you aren't ever going to make me into a silent woman."

Once again everyone laughed and within minutes the men had returned to the great room while the women cleared the table. "One of these days we're going to make them stay here and do the dishes while we go into the other room and relax," Edie said as she began rinsing dishes and handing them to Peyton, who placed them in the dishwasher.

"You know they would do the dishes if any of you asked them to," Brittany said.

Portia smiled. "And that's exactly why we don't ask them to. We all let them pretend to be the big macho men, but we also know that underneath all that bluster are pussycats with tender hearts."

That perfectly described the Grayson men and someday Brittany wanted to find a man like her brothers, a man who could protect her against the world if she needed it and who would love her to distraction.

It was after dark when the gathering began to break up. Edie looped arms with Brittany as she walked out the front door. "You want to spend the night here?" she asked. "Maybe you'd sleep better here than you've been doing at home."

The offer definitely held more than a little bit of appeal, but Brittany shook her head. "Thanks for the offer, but I'd rather go home." It felt too much like going backward to spend the night here where she'd stayed for her months of recuperation.

"Are you sure you're doing okay?" Edie asked. Benjamin and Edie had spent the most time with her after she'd been rescued. Edie had sat up with her many a night when she was afraid to sleep for fear of the nightmares that might plague her.

"Am I back to normal? No, but I'm doing okay." She gave Edie a forced smile. "Logically I know that he's dead and I have nothing more to fear, but emotionally I haven't quite embraced the notion of safety just yet."

Edie gave her a warm hug. "You never wanted to talk much about the time you were held, but you know if you ever need to talk I'm here for you."

Brittany returned the hug. "I know. And now I'm going to head home and hope for a good night's sleep."

Minutes later as she drove home, she thought about those months she'd been held. She hadn't shared a lot with her family about that time, not wanting to burden them with the details. Although physically she hadn't been molested or beaten, the mental abuse had been horrific.

The Professional had made sure she'd had enough water and food to stay alive, but he'd taunted her with all the terrible things he was going to do to her. Each time the door to the shed had swung open, she'd feared that it was the moment of her death, a horrible and painful death.

And in that place of fear, in that horrible space of

abject terror, Brittany had found the utter darkness in her heart, the depth of her shame.

"But you're going to be fine," she said aloud as she gripped the steering wheel more firmly. The danger was over and life could only get better and better from this minute onward.

What she didn't understand was why no matter how many times she told herself this, no matter how badly she wanted to believe it, there was still a part of her that was terrified that the bad times weren't over yet.

The house was clean, Emily had gone to spend the night with Rose, and the steaks were marinating and ready to pop in the broiler. Everything was ready for dinner with Brittany, except that Alex was more nervous than he had been in a very long time.

He'd spent the day at her house working on the deck with Buck and Gary but Brittany had kept herself scarce, only coming out once in the afternoon to bring them all lemonade.

He now glanced at his watch. Almost six-thirty. She should be here anytime now and he told himself it was ridiculous to be so nervous about a simple dinner with a friend.

A friend, that's all she was going to be, he told himself. A beautiful friend with eyes he wanted to drown in, with a tragic past he wished he could fix. Jeez, he needed to get his emotions where she was concerned under control.

Still, when the doorbell rang he nearly jumped out of his skin. He opened the door and the sight of her instantly calmed his nerves. She looked lovely in a pair of brown slacks and a yellow blouse that enhanced the darkness of her hair and eyes. She also looked nervous and that strangely put him at ease. She clutched her purse tightly to her chest and her smile was tentative.

"No need to look so terrified. I promise I won't bite," he said.

Her features relaxed and her smile grew more natural. "I know it's crazy, but I am feeling a bit nervous," she admitted.

"It doesn't sound crazy. I was feeling the same way just a minute ago." He gestured her toward the living room. "Maybe a glass of wine will make us both relax."

"That sounds nice," she agreed.

He walked her through the living room and into the kitchen where the table was already set for two and a salad and a loaf of warmed French bread sat in the center.

"Where's Emily?" she asked as he gestured her into one of the chairs at the table.

"I packed her off to Rose's for the night." He pulled a bottle of red wine from the refrigerator and smiled. "I love my daughter to distraction, but sometimes I get hungry for adult conversation. Besides, she and Rose have been working on some intricate 3-D puzzle at Rose's house. Lately I've had trouble keeping Emily home."

He poured them each a glass of wine and then carried hers to the table. "And now the most important question of the night—how do you like your steak?"

She set her purse on the floor next to her chair and took the wineglass from him. "Medium."

He placed the steaks in the oven and then joined her at the table, and for a moment an awkward silence descended, broken when they both started to say something at the same time.

"Sorry," she said with a small laugh. "I was just going to say that it was my sister-in-law who sold you this house."

"Layla? She's a nice woman," he replied.

"She talks a lot," Brittany replied with a small grin.

Alex laughed and felt the ice breaking between them. "Yeah, even Emily said that Layla was a bit of a chatterbox, and if that isn't the pot calling the kettle black I don't know what is."

Brittany laughed and then took a sip of the wine and eyed him soberly over the rim of the glass. "It must be hard, to be a man raising a little girl."

"It has its moments," he agreed. "It took me months to learn to paint her fingernails to her approval and I still can't get the hang of a French braid. Actually, I'm lucky that she's a great kid and is very patient with me."

"I could help you out with the French-braid thing," she replied.

"Emily would be ecstatic."

She nodded and took another sip of the wine. "The deck seems to be coming along faster than I'd expected."

"There's still a lot to do. Getting the floor down is

the easy part. The railings and finish work take a bit longer."

"Have you used Buck and Gary before as helpers?"

"Buck, yes, Gary, no. Buck helped me on a previous job and I told him I wouldn't mind hiring another kid to help with the grunt work and he suggested Gary."

"I don't know if you know this or not, but Buck has quite a reputation."

He smiled. "One thing I've learned since moving here is that the people of Black Rock like to gossip and nobody is shy about having opinions. I try not to listen to rumors and I like to judge people on their own merits."

"I'm sure you've heard more than a little gossip about me."

"A little," he agreed.

She gazed down into her wineglass and when she looked back at him her eyes were filled with a steely strength. "I was kidnapped by a crazy serial killer and held captive in an old shed for four months. During that time he kidnapped four more women and planned to torture and kill us each, one at a time. He called it a party. Thankfully we were all rescued before he could have his little party. I survived and it's just something that happened to me. It's in my past now."

A wealth of respect for her washed over him. "Must have been terrible."

"It was. But so are cancer and plane crashes and a thousand other things that happen in the world."

"What happened to the other women who were kidnapped?"

She took a sip of her wine and then answered, "They've all left town, except Layla. Suzy Bakersfield moved away with her boyfriend. Casey Teasdale married her fiancé and they also left town, and Jennifer Hightower went to live with an aunt in New York. Layla was the last one to be kidnapped and I like to think that if my brothers hadn't rescued us when they did she would have talked Larry Norwood to death before he managed to kill her."

Alex smiled and then jumped up from the table to check on the steaks. He flipped them over and then returned to his seat. "You know, I've been thinking about what you said to me the other night."

She frowned. "What was that?"

"That you don't go into town because people stare at you and whisper behind your back. I was thinking maybe if you went into town more often people would get used to seeing you around again and the stares and whispers would stop."

She cocked her head as if giving it some thought. "Maybe you're right," she finally agreed. "I think it wouldn't have been so bad if the other women were still around, but I was the one who was held the longest and so people seem to be the most curious about what I went through."

"And you'd just rather put it behind you and not talk about it," he said.

She flashed him a beatific smile. "That's right."

"I just want you to know one thing—if you need it, I can be a sympathetic ear or a comforting shoulder."

Her eyes flared with a sliver of evocative heat that

he felt deep inside. "Thanks," she replied. "I'll keep that in mind."

He wanted to kiss her. At that moment with her eyes shining so bright and her lips moist from the wine, he wanted to take her into his arms and lose himself in a kiss. Instead he jumped up from the table and went back to the oven where he pulled the steaks out.

"Is there anything I can do to help?" she asked.

"No, thanks, I'm all set." He plated the steaks and then carried them to the table.

Thankfully the dinner conversation flowed easily. He regaled her with stories about his days as an attorney in Chicago, enjoying each time he managed to make her laugh.

In turn, she told him about growing up with four older brothers who teased and spoiled her unmercifully. "When I told Tom I wanted to become a deputy he fought me tooth and nail," she said. "There was no way he wanted his baby sister on the streets with a gun."

"So, how did you convince him to hire you?" Alex asked, half-mesmerized by the sheen of her dark hair beneath the artificial light overhead. He knew it would feel like silk between his fingers, imagined the long strands whispering against his bare chest as she straddled him.

"I told him if he didn't hire me then I was sure Topeka or Wichita would be willing to take me on. He hated the idea of me being on those streets even more, so he gave me the job here."

"And you liked being a deputy?" he asked, trying to stay focused on the conversation instead of on her physical attributes.

She didn't answer for a long moment. "I did, but I think I'm ready for a change now. I'm not sure that being a deputy was a true calling for me." She looked away from him and he got the feeling that she didn't completely believe her own words.

"That's the way I felt about being a lawyer. I went into the profession because I knew it would provide a good living for my family, but my true love has always been building things with my hands."

"I'm not sure where my heart lies at the moment," she said as she reached for a piece of the bread. "I enjoy working on the computer and have gotten pretty good at making web pages." Her cheeks flushed a charming pink. "In the months after the crime when I was staying out at my brother's ranch, I was most comfortable social networking with cyber friends and teaching myself the ins and outs of web design."

"If you decide you want to do that, I'll gladly be your first client. I need to get a web page up to advertise my remodeling work. I'd love to hire you."

She smiled at him. "I think we can work something out."

With dinner finished she insisted she help with the cleanup, even though he told her she should sit and enjoy being a guest.

They worked well together, as if they'd cleaned up after dinner together a hundred times before. Afterward he poured them each another glass of wine and they went into the living room.

"You have a lovely home," she said as she sank down on one end of the sofa and he sat on the other end.

"Thanks, it's finally starting to feel like home."

Once again she studied him over the rim of her glass, her eyes dark and unreadable. "How did your wife die?"

"Breast cancer."

"That's rotten," she replied.

He took a deep swallow of the wine and then set his glass on the coffee table. "What was really rotten was that she knew she had a lump in her breast for months but she didn't tell me about it and she didn't go to the doctor." He heard the edge of anger that had crept into his voice.

"Why?"

He leaned back against the sofa cushion. "We had a whirlwind romance. I met her at a fundraiser and within six months we were married. Don't get me wrong, I loved her, but it wasn't long into the marriage that I realized she was more child than woman, and by the time she got pregnant with Emily any passion I'd felt for her was gone. She was fragile, afraid of her own shadow, and it only got worse when Emily was born. By the time she finally told me about the lump the cancer had spread everywhere. She was gone within six months."

To his surprise Brittany leaned over and touched his hand, a gentle touch that lasted only a moment before she pulled away. "I'm sorry. That must have been horrible."

"It was tragic," he replied. "She didn't have to die, but she was so afraid of living that was the choice she made. If I ever decide to marry again, and I'm not sure I will, I'd want a strong woman who isn't afraid of life."

He frowned, realizing he'd said far more than he'd intended to say about Linda…about his previous life. "Sorry, I must be boring you to death."

"Not at all," she replied quickly enough that he believed her. "It's just a reminder that life can be so unpredictable, that you have to grasp your happiness whenever you can."

For the next two hours they talked about favorite movies and food, sharing little tidbits of information to get to know each other better. And everything Alex heard from her made him like her more and more. She was funny and bright and beautiful, and as the evening drew to a close he wasn't ready for it to end.

"I'll walk you home," he said as he opened the front door and realized darkness had fallen while they'd talked.

"That isn't necessary," she protested but her eyes darkened a little as she stared outside into the night.

"It might not be necessary, but I wouldn't be a true gentleman if I let you walk home alone in the dark, and I definitely want you to think of me as a gentleman."

Brittany slung her purse strap over her shoulder and smiled. "Okay, then."

As they stepped out onto his porch he locked the door and pulled it shut behind them. "This has been really nice," she said as they started down his walk.

"Yes, it has," he agreed. The scent of flowers rose up to him, but didn't diminish the scent of her that had teased him all night long.

He'd told her he was just interested in having a friend, some companionship to fill the lonely hours of the day, but after spending the evening with her he recognized he wanted more from her.

She was so different from the wife he'd lost, so filled with life and with that core of inner strength that radiated from her eyes. She drew him, stirring a simmering passion that he hadn't expected.

"I was serious about that web page," he said when they reached her porch. "I'd like to hire you to get one up and running for me." They stopped at her door.

In the faint spill of light from a nearby streetlamp, her eyes glowed as she gazed up at him. "Are you sure you aren't just trying to be nice?"

He grinned at her. "I'm a lawyer. When it comes to business I'm not nice—I'm a shark."

She laughed, that low throaty sound that swirled warmth inside his belly. "Okay, then, why don't I work something up tomorrow while you're working on the deck and before you knock off for the day we can talk about it?" She turned and unlocked her front door.

"Sounds like a plan," he agreed.

"Thank you, Alex, for a terrific night."

"No, thank you."

For a long moment they remained standing far too

close together, their gazes locked. He realized he intended to kiss her and saw the dawning realization take hold of her, as well.

He took a step toward her and she didn't retreat. Instead she raised her chin, her lips parted slightly as if to welcome him.

He took the subtle invitation, gathering her into his arms as his mouth met hers. He'd intended only a sweet, soft good-night kiss, but her lips held a heat that transformed his intent, his initial desire.

Pulling her closer, he deepened the kiss, tentatively touching his tongue to hers. Her arms wrapped around his neck as she returned the kiss, leaning into him in surrender.

He wasn't sure who broke the kiss, he or she, but they broke apart and she gave a shaky laugh. "I'm not used to my friends kissing me like that."

"Sorry," he replied. "I don't usually kiss my friends that way."

"Don't apologize. It was the perfect ending to a perfect night."

Before he could reply she was gone, leaving him staring at the sight of her closed front door and with a well of want inside him that stole his breath away.

As he started back down the sidewalk toward his house he realized there was no way he'd be satisfied with Brittany just being his friend.

He tried to tamp down the pleasure that coursed through him. He'd misjudged a woman before and wasn't eager to make the same kind of mistake.

Alex didn't believe in happily-ever-after anymore and it was going to take more than a scorching kiss with a hot woman to change his mind.

Chapter 4

The kiss had shaken her to her very core. Alex was the wrong man for her for a million reasons. She wasn't ready for a relationship. He had a daughter and she wasn't mother material. And yet for all the reasons he was wrong for her, the kiss had felt so right.

She stood at the window and watched the men working on the deck, her gaze lingering on the man who had rocked her world with a single kiss the night before.

Each time she thought about it her mouth tingled with pleasure and her entire body enjoyed a wash of warmth that made her want to repeat the experience.

It had just been a kiss, but it had made her want more and that worried her just a little bit. Wrong man, she kept trying to remind herself.

She'd learned as much about him with the things he hadn't said as what he had shared with her. His marriage had obviously not been great, but she was certain that if his wife hadn't died he would have remained in the marriage, taking care of a fragile wife and his daughter. She instinctively knew he was the kind of man who would sacrifice his own happiness for that of his family.

He deserved better than her. She was a spoiled brat who, before her kidnapping, hadn't thought about anyone but herself and if that weren't enough she still had some baggage left from her ordeal.

She turned away from the window with a sigh and sat at the table where her laptop was open. As she waited for it to power up, she thought about her work as a deputy. She'd fibbed to Alex. She'd absolutely loved being a deputy, but just like the crime had changed her, it had also changed what she thought she could be in the future.

Once the computer was up and running she got to work. When Alex had arrived that morning he'd brought with him a sheet of paper with all the pertinent details necessary to build him a web page.

She consciously shoved away the memory of his kiss and instead focused on the task at hand. As always it didn't take her long to lose herself in cyberspace.

She stopped at noon to fix herself a quick sandwich. A glance out the back window let her know that apparently Alex and the others had also knocked off for lunch.

By the time she'd finished her lunch the three men were back to work in the yard and once again she found herself wandering to the window. She told herself it was to watch the progress being made on her deck, but she couldn't stop her gaze from lingering on Alex.

What was it about him that drew her? Physically it was an easy question to answer, but it wasn't just physical attraction she felt for him. Certainly she liked the way his smile flashed his straight white teeth against his tanned skin, and the width of his shoulders made her want to get lost in his embrace.

But it was the man she sensed beneath the handsome package that drew her, a man who loved his daughter enough to quit his job and move across the country so she could have a loving grandmother in her life, a man who from what little he'd said about his own parents hadn't had a solid support system while growing up.

From what he'd told her his parents had been in their mid-thirties when they'd had him. He'd been an oops baby and by the time he was six he realized his parents weren't cut out to be real parents. He'd become a self-reliant child who had matured into a self-reliant man.

With a muttered curse of frustration she returned to her work on the computer. By the time three o'clock came and Alex knocked on the back door to let her know they were stopping work for the day, she had a tentative site to show him.

He leaned over the back of her to view the monitor

and the scent of him coupled with his body heat made her heart flutter.

"That looks great," he exclaimed. "It's exactly what I had in mind. You're obviously very talented at this."

Pleasure washed over her. "I'm still learning, but I do enjoy it. All we need to do is set you up with a domain name and a hosting service and we can get it published to the internet."

"Can you take care of all that?" he asked as she got up to walk him to the front door. "Add it into your fee?"

"Sure, I can do that," she agreed.

They reached her front door and he turned back to face her. "I was thinking maybe after dinner tonight you could give me that lesson in French braiding? Emily would be thrilled if she could have her hair done for school tomorrow."

"Sure, that would be fine," she agreed.

"How about around six-thirty?"

"Sounds good."

It was only after he left that she wondered if maybe things were moving too fast. She'd already figured out all the reasons why she was wrong for him. Still, she didn't want to disappoint Emily by reneging on the offer now.

And if she were perfectly honest with herself she would admit that she wouldn't mind the company. The evening hours were the worst for her, when the dark shadows of night began to spill over everything, over her.

It was precisely six-thirty when Alex and Emily

returned to her house. Brittany opened the door and Emily danced in and immediately threw her arms around her waist.

"Thank you, thank you!" she exclaimed. "I've been telling daddy for a long time that I'm too old for pigtails and I need a French braid, but he's having such trouble and needs your help."

Brittany was stunned by how much the hug warmed her. Emily smelled of bubble bath and innocence, and Brittany returned the hug with one of her own. "By the time you leave here tonight your daddy will be able to French braid in his sleep," she promised.

She straightened and smiled at Alex. "Come on, we have work to do." She led them into the living room where she had laid out a brush and comb on the coffee table in preparation for playing beauty shop.

"I washed my hair and everything," Emily said. "And when you're all finished with me, Daddy is going to take me to grandma's to show her how beautiful I look."

"Honey, you're beautiful without a French braid," Brittany replied. She sat on the sofa and patted the space next to her. "Let's put Daddy here and you sit on the floor here in front of me."

Brittany was far too aware of Alex as he sank down next to her. His body heat wrapped around her, as well as the scent of his spicy cologne. As she picked up the hairbrush, she felt ridiculously clumsy, as if she'd suddenly grown ten thumbs.

She began to brush through Emily's hair, enjoying the feel of the pale, silky strands. "My mommy used to brush my hair like this," Emily said as she relaxed against Brittany's legs.

Brittany's heart squeezed for Emily's loss. "I'll bet you miss that," she said as she exchanged a quick glance with Alex.

"Sometimes, but Daddy tries his best and he's getting better and better," Emily replied. "He only pulls sometimes if he gets in too much of a hurry, but he's always sorry when he does."

"That's good. And now, for the fine art of French braiding." As she began to braid Emily's hair she went slowly, showing Alex exactly how it was done. He watched intently, as if it was the most important thing he might learn for the rest of his life, and that made Brittany only like him more.

"Okay," she said when she was finished. "Now we're going to take it all out and let you try."

Alex looked at her dubiously. Emily turned around and flashed him a bright smile. "Don't worry, Daddy. I know you can do it," she said as she scooted over in front of him.

Brittany could never have guessed that a lesson in braiding hair could become a study in sexual tension, but as she leaned against Alex and guided his fingers through Emily's hair, tension coiled in her stomach as she wondered what those fingers of his would feel like sliding through her own hair, over her bare skin.

She could tell he felt it, too. When his gaze met hers his eyes were darker in hue, simmering with a hunger that was unmistakable.

By the time she'd had him work the hair three times

in a row, she felt as if he knew what he was doing and she rose from the sofa, needing to distance herself from him. "Emily, want to see in the mirror?" she asked the little girl.

"Oh, yes," Emily exclaimed with eagerness as she got up from the floor.

Brittany led her into her bedroom where she had a full-length mirror on the back of the door. Emily gazed at her reflection and emitted a little squeal. "It's perfect."

It wasn't perfect, but it was a terrific effort by a terrific dad. Emily turned and looked at Brittany. "Would you like me to brush your hair? Sometimes I brushed my mommy's hair for her and since you did mine I could do yours."

The offer touched Brittany deeply. "That's very nice, Emily, but I think my hair is just fine for tonight."

"Okay, then I'll owe you one," Emily replied. She turned back to the mirror and gazed at her reflection. "Do I look older?"

Brittany hid her smile and studied the little girl thoughtfully. "You know, I think you do. With your hair like that you look at least eight."

Emily preened. "Now we have to go show my grandma," she said as they left Brittany's bedroom.

Alex stood in the middle of the living room, his gaze unfathomable as it lingered on Brittany. "Thanks," he said simply.

She smiled and nodded. "Not a problem."

"Brittany, you want to come with us to visit my

grandma? She's going to be so surprised. She couldn't braid my hair because she has bad fingers that hurt."

"Arthritis," Alex said.

"Thank you for the invitation, Emily, but maybe another time," Brittany replied.

"That sounds like a plan," Emily replied.

Alex checked his watch. "And we'd better get over there if we're going so we can get you back home and in bed on time for school tomorrow."

When they reached the door Emily gave her another hug and Alex thanked her once again, the heat still lingering in his gaze.

She felt that heat long after they'd left and she was once again alone. She picked up her hairbrush and comb and carried them back into her bathroom, her head filled with thoughts of both Emily and her daddy.

The fact that Emily had even offered to brush Brittany's hair let her know that Emily was kind and thoughtful, and Brittany knew that was a testimony to Alex's great parenting.

But it wasn't his parenting skills that coiled heat in the pit of her stomach and made her think about rumpled sheets and his scent lingering on her pillowcase.

She somehow felt as if she were on a runaway train where he was concerned, powerless to halt the careening forward motion. *But do you really want to stop it?* a small voice whispered inside her head as she turned on the television and settled in on the sofa.

Would it be so terrible to follow through on the desire she felt for Alex? To have a wild and passionate relationship with him? It didn't have to mean anything. It didn't have to lead to some attempt to build something lasting.

She wouldn't actively pursue a physical relationship with Alex, she decided, but if it happened spontaneously she wasn't sure she would try to stop it.

As far as Emily went, there was no reason she couldn't be friendly with the little girl. It wasn't as if she was auditioning to become a stepmother. They were neighbors and there was no reason they couldn't share an occasional trip to Izzy's or maybe even have lunch together.

A feeling of peace swept through Brittany, a peace that had been missing for a long time. For the first time in months she felt as if she were finally returning to the land of the living and it felt wonderful.

When Alex looked at her she didn't feel like a freak—she felt like a desirable, normal woman. He didn't treat her as if she was a fragile victim of a horrendous crime. He appeared to only have an interest in the woman she was now, and that was definitely more than a little bit heady.

She watched TV for an hour, then bored with what was on the tube, she went back into the kitchen where her laptop was still on the kitchen table.

The computer work would always be a hobby she enjoyed, but her true calling had been working the streets of Black Rock with a badge on her chest. It was one more thing The Professional had taken away from her. She no longer felt competent to wear the badge.

In the darkness of the shed, with the chilling voice of The Professional taunting and teasing her with promises of such heinous things, she'd contemplated what no deputy should ever contemplate.

Shoving these thoughts aside, she logged in to her social-networking page and for the next hour read innocuous messages from people she had never met. She rarely posted on the page, instead just reading messages and posts from friends and friends of friends.

Reading the mundane tidbits of those lives helped fill the hours before bedtime and made her feel a little connected to the outside world.

She surfed the internet until just after nine, then powered down her computer and got up to carry her soda glass to the sink. As she gazed up at the window her heart slammed against her ribs and the glass crashed to the bottom of the sink.

It was him!

The Professional.

He stared at her through the window glass, his face covered with the familiar black ski mask. His eyes glittered the way she remembered, with evil intent. This was the way she saw him in her nightmares.

For what felt like an eternity she was frozen, locked in a hellish gaze with the man who had nearly taken her life, the man who had stolen her innocence and sense of self.

The moment lasted only a moment, broken by the scream that crawled up her throat as she reeled backward and crashed into the table.

She went down hard on her butt on the floor, skittering backward like a crab on hot sand to escape. He was back! The face. That masked face. She had to get away.

She managed to get to her feet and half ran, half stumbled into the living room. Terror gripped her by the neck, trapping the scream as her throat constricted painfully.

Grabbing the phone from the end table, she sobbed as it took her two times to punch in her brother Tom's phone number. She found her voice when he answered and sobbed his name. "He's here. The Professional is here. Please hurry…hurry!"

Someplace in the back of her mind she knew it would take him too long to come. She needed help now, before The Professional somehow got inside the house, before he had the party he'd promised and hadn't had a chance to deliver.

There was only one other phone number in her head, the one that had been on the contact information Alex had given her earlier in the day to aid her in building his web page. She punched it in, and gasped in relief as he answered on the second ring.

"Alex, can you come to my house right now? There's somebody outside. I'm scared."

"I'll be right there," he replied.

She remained clutching the phone after he'd hung up, listening for the sound of a shattering window, a broken door that would indicate that The Professional had gained entry into her home.

It wasn't done. It wasn't over. She'd known in her heart, in her very soul that it wasn't finished yet. Now all she could do was hope and pray that somebody would get here before The Professional had his final party with her.

Thankfully Emily had decided to spend the night with Rose, and Alex was still dressed when he got Brittany's call. He grabbed his house keys and tore down the sidewalk, keeping an eye on his surroundings as he looked for a possible intruder in the area.

She'd been terrified. He'd heard it in her voice. Whoever she'd seen had positively scared her to death and the fear in her voice had sliced through him like a knife.

He saw nobody and when he reached Brittany's house he knocked on the front door. There was no reply. He knocked again, harder, and called out her name. "Brittany, it's me, Alex."

The door flew open and she launched herself into his arms, her slender body trembling uncontrollably as she began to weep. "Hey, it's okay," he said. "You're okay now." He moved her into the house and closed and locked the door behind him, but she refused to leave his arms.

"He was here," she said between sobs, her voice slightly muffled as she buried her head in the front of his shirt. "He came back for me. It's not over. I thought it was over, but it's not."

"Who? Honey, tell me what happened."

She shook her head and burrowed closer against him, her sobs ripping from deep in her throat in despair. He didn't try to talk to her again. He just held her until her sobs became softer and finally stopped altogether.

He'd just led her to the sofa to sit when the doorbell rang. "That should be my brother Tom," she said as she swiped the last of the tears from her cheeks.

Alex answered the door to a tall, dark-haired man who had the same coloring as and, although bolder and more masculine, similar features to Brittany. "Alex Crawford," he said in introduction. "I'm Brittany's neighbor."

"Tom Grayson," he replied. "Sheriff Tom Grayson." He walked in to where Brittany remained on the sofa, her arms around herself as if seeking some sort of warmth. "What happened?" He eased down next to his sister as Alex stood nearby.

"He was here." The words were a bare whisper as they left her lips. She looked up at her brother, her brown eyes wide and still filled with terror. "The Professional."

Tom exchanged a dark glance with Alex. "Brittany, you know that isn't possible. Larry Norwood is dead. Larry was The Professional and he's no longer on this earth. He died in that shed. He can't hurt you anymore."

She shook her head. "He's back. I saw him. He was staring at me through my kitchen window just a few minutes ago." Her voice was filled with vehemence.

"What did he look like?" Tom asked.

"He was wearing a black ski mask, just like Larry used to wear. His eyes…his eyes glittered with that sick excitement, with that horrible evil." A shiver worked through her and she tightened her arms around her shoulders.

Tom got up from the sofa and for the first time Alex noticed the man had his gun strapped to his waist even though he wasn't in uniform, clad in a pair of worn jeans and a short-sleeved navy shirt. "I'll go out and take a look around."

Without waiting for a reply he left the house by the front door. Brittany began to tremble once again and Alex moved back to the sofa to take her into his arms.

"You're okay now," he murmured against her sweet-smelling hair. "Nobody is going to hurt you."

"I just looked up and he was there, staring at me through the window. It was like a vision from a nightmare, a horrible nightmare."

He tightened his arms around her. He had no idea what had happened, but he knew true terror when he saw it, when he felt it trembling in his arms, and whatever Brittany had seen had definitely terrified her.

Within minutes Tom was back, his gaze inscrutable. "I didn't see anyone and there are no signs that anyone was back there." He stuffed his hands into his pockets and stared at his sister, who sat up and moved away from Alex's embrace.

"Are you sure maybe you didn't see your own reflection in the window and freak out?" he asked.

Brittany's back went rigid. "My own reflection usually doesn't scare me." She shook her head. "I know what I saw and it was a man in a ski mask."

"But it wasn't The Professional," Tom countered.

Brittany hesitated a moment. "Of course, you're

right. Larry Norwood is dead, but somebody was out-side my window, somebody wearing a ski mask just like Larry used to do when he came into the shed."

She got up from the sofa and walked over to her brother. "Somebody is after me, Tom. I feel it. I know it in the very depth of my being. It's not over yet for me and I'm afraid."

Tom hesitated a moment and then released a deep sigh. "Maybe you should talk to somebody about post-traumatic stress."

"I'm not crazy. I saw what I saw," she exclaimed with rising anger in her voice.

"Well, there's nobody out there now and if it will make you feel better I'll have Caleb do extra drive-bys through the night," he replied. "Or if you'd feel better you can come home with me."

"No, thanks," she said stiffly. "I'll stay here, but I would appreciate the extra patrols."

Alex could tell Brittany was angry and she re-mained so as she ushered her brother out the front door. She whirled back around to face Alex. "I suppose you think I'm crazy, too?"

Alex wasn't sure what he believed, but he was a smart man and knew what she needed just now was somebody on her side. "Of course not," he replied.

She stared at him for a few seconds, then her shoulders sagged forward and she returned to the sofa and sank down. "I know what I saw," she said more to herself than to him. "I'm certain of what I saw." Her hands clenched into fists in her lap.

"I believe you saw somebody," he said as he sat next

to her. "And I believe he was wearing a ski mask, but we both know it wasn't The Professional."

She drew a deep breath and nodded. "In that first moment of fear when I saw him, that's all I could think about, that somehow he'd returned from the grave to finish what he'd started. But I know that's crazy." Her hands had relaxed in her lap and he took one of them in his.

"Maybe somebody is playing a very sick joke on you," he suggested.

"Maybe," she admitted as a tiny frown appeared in the center of her forehead. "There was the balloon the other day."

It was Alex's turn to frown. "The balloon?"

"Remember, the day you came to see about the deck there was a red balloon tied to my mailbox."

"I remember," he replied. "But I'm not sure I understand what a red balloon has to do with all of this."

She leaned her head back against the sofa cushion, her gaze suddenly distant. "On that last day, in the final moments before he was going to kill us all, he released a handful of red balloons to celebrate the start of his 'party.' They were like blood droplets floating upward." She shivered, as if the memory chilled her to the bone.

Alex squeezed her hand in an attempt to bring her back from the bad place she'd gone to in her memory. "But you survived and Larry Norwood is dead and now we need to figure out who might be doing these things to you." He squeezed her hand once again and then released it. "Is there anyone you can think of who might want to torment you? Or maybe somebody who might think something like this is funny?"

"No," she replied immediately. "I can't imagine anyone who would want to do something so cruel or would have such a sick sense of humor."

"Who might know about the details of what happened with you and The Professional?" he asked.

She got up from the sofa and released a small, humorless laugh. "Only everyone in town. There are no secrets in Black Rock. I guarantee five minutes after we were all taken out of that shed every detail of what had happened in there was known to everyone in town."

"But there's somebody in town who apparently is using those facts to taunt you," he replied as he also rose from the sofa.

Her features suddenly reflected a new horror. "Where's Emily?"

"Don't worry. She spent the night with Rose tonight."

"Thank God," she gasped in relief. "For a minute I thought maybe you'd left her at home all alone."

He smiled. "She's fine. And now I want to make sure you're fine. Would you like me to stay here tonight? Spend the night on your sofa? Or maybe you'd rather come to my place for the rest of the night? I've got a spare bedroom where you'd be comfortable."

She hesitated only a moment and then shook her head. "Thanks, but I'll be fine here. I have good locks on the door and Tom said there's nobody around here now. Caleb is going to do drive-bys so the excitement for the night is probably over."

"Are you sure you're okay here alone?" he asked. He still didn't know if there was any real danger to her, but the last thing he wanted was for her to spend the night in fear.

"Yes, really, I'm fine now." She looked better. The color was back in her cheeks and she'd stopped trembling. She offered him a tight smile. "It was nice of you to come running when I called."

"Anytime, Brittany. Anytime day or night if you need me I'll be here. The last thing I want is for you to be alone and afraid."

Her gaze was soft as it lingered on him. She walked to where he stood and stretched up and kissed him on his cheek. "Thank you, Alex. Thank you for believing me and thank you for being here for me."

She stepped back from him, precluding any idea he might have had of taking her in his arms for a deeper, more intimate embrace. "I'll see you in the morning."

"If you need anything more tonight, just give me a call," he said as they walked to the front door.

"Thanks, but I'm sure I'll be fine now."

A moment later as Alex headed back toward his house, he wondered about the truth of what had happened tonight. It had been obvious that Brittany's brother Tom hadn't believed there had been somebody at the window, that he thought his sister was suffering some sort of post-traumatic stress disorder.

Certainly the balloon he'd seen tied to her mailbox had been real, but there could be a dozen logical ex-

planations for that and none of them included a killer
rising up from the dead.

Was it possible that Brittany was much more fragile
than he'd initially believed? It had been her strength
that had first drawn him to her, but was that strength
merely a facade hiding a flaw that was the legacy of
what she'd been through? Was she not the strong survivor he'd thought her to be?

With the feel of her kiss warming his cheek, he now
felt as if his most important decision to make was if
he should invite her into his life, into Emily's life in a
meaningful way or if perhaps the best thing he could
do for himself and his daughter would be to cut his
losses and run.

Chapter 5

"I'm not crazy. I'm not!" Brittany said aloud to herself as she locked the door after Alex left. She didn't care what her brother thought. She didn't care what anyone thought. It hadn't been her own reflection she'd seen in the window and it hadn't been a figment of her imagination.

There had been somebody there, and his eyes had sparked with malevolence. There had been somebody there, hadn't there? She sank down on the sofa and buried her face in her hands, a wild despair sweeping through her. *Maybe you are crazy,* a little voice whispered in the back of her brain.

Tears burned at her eyes at the torture of that small voice. What if she truly had imagined the face at the window? What if the trauma that she'd suffered at the hands of The Professional had left her teetering on the brink of insanity?

Her brothers certainly thought that's what had happened, that she was jumping at shadows and imagining danger behind every bush. They all thought she could use some therapy, and maybe she could, but that didn't make her believe she'd only imagined that face at the window.

She'd hated the fact that what she'd seen in Tom's eyes had been a touch of pity, more than a little compassion for somebody who might be sick. She hadn't missed the look he'd exchanged with Alex.

She'd never felt as alone as she did now. Had Alex believed her or had he just been being kind? She wasn't sure. When she'd asked him he'd replied that he believed she thought she saw something. That didn't mean that he believed somebody had really been there.

One thing was certain. Although in those first moments of sheer panic she'd believed somehow, someway Larry Norwood had come back for her, now that some of the panic had worn off she knew it wasn't possible that it had been Larry.

Larry was dead and she knew he could never hurt her again, but somebody was playing with her and she didn't know the rules of the game. What's more, nobody else apparently knew or believed that a game was being played with her.

And if it was a game, then what was the object? She shook her head and swiped her tears from her cheeks. Maybe she was making too much of everything. The balloon could have been from a birthday party on the street and the man staring into her kitchen window might have been nothing more than a Peeping Tom.

Every town had a Peeping Tom. Bored teenagers sneaking around in the night, a pervert trying to catch a glimpse of a woman in a state of undress. Generally speaking, Peeping Toms were harmless.

She certainly could live with the fact that she'd overreacted, but the idea that she was somehow losing her mind was terrifying.

Knowing that sleep would be impossible for some time to come, she got up from the sofa, went to the front window and peered out just in time to see a patrol car slowly passing her house. A brilliant light shone on the bushes by her porch, then across the front of the house itself. Caleb was taking his job seriously.

Tom had been as good as his word and a new feeling of safety swept through her. Besides, it wasn't as if the masked man had tried to break the window. He'd simply been looking at her—like some perverted peeper.

With each moment that passed, the terror she'd felt began to ebb away, leaving her with only a weary exhaustion. It was after eleven and even though an hour ago she hadn't thought she'd ever be able to sleep again, she now stifled a yawn.

Maybe a nice hot cup of tea would finish relaxing her enough that she could sleep without nightmares of what had been, without worries about what might be. She didn't want to go to sleep believing that she was slowly but surely losing her mind or that some faceless, nameless evil was after her once again.

She filled up a teakettle, preferring the traditional way to make tea to the microwave. With the water on the stove, she sank back down at the table, her gaze going to the window above the sink.

Had there been somebody there? She'd been so certain, but now doubts were slowly creeping in. There was no question that she'd been on edge lately.

She loved being back in her own space, back in the home that she'd dreamed of while being held captive. She'd bought the house two years before and each stick of furniture, every dish towel and knickknack had been chosen with care to create her own comfortable nest.

She hated the fact that the face at the window had momentarily shaken the safety, the security she'd always felt here.

The whistle of the teakettle pulled her from her thoughts. She moved it off the burner and then grabbed a teacup from the cabinet.

With her raspberry tea made she sat at the table and thought about the events of the night. It had definitely been a roller-coaster ride. She'd been surprised to find that she'd enjoyed her time with Emily. The little girl was easy to be around, delightful in a natural way.

But was it right for Brittany to get any closer to her when she might be losing her mind? She took a sip of her tea, muttering a curse beneath her breath as she burned her bottom lip on the hot, fragrant brew.

Certainly Alex and Emily had been through enough heartache in their lives. The last thing they needed around them was a woman afraid that a serial killer was somehow stalking her from his grave.

Perhaps the light from the moon had made some weird reflection in the window. Maybe she'd been stressing more than she'd realized and the stress had made her momentarily snap and see a phantom.

She finished her tea and with a sigh got up from the table. A good night's sleep would put everything into perspective. Still, as she carried her cup to the sink her heart tap-danced a slightly faster rhythm than normal.

But as she approached the back window, there was nothing there except a faint cast of moonlight illuminating the partially finished deck. No masked man, no killer from the dead—just a backyard shrouded with the shadows of night.

As she rinsed her cup and placed it in the dishwasher her heart continued the accelerated beat. What if she had hallucinated the face in the window? What if her mind was slipping?

In the four months that she had been a prisoner in a small cell in a shed, that had been one of her fears, that she would slowly go out of her mind.

It would definitely be ironic if she had survived everything that The Professional had put her through only to lose herself to madness now. That's not happening, she told herself firmly as she turned away from the dishwasher.

That's when she saw it. A folded piece of paper stuck beneath her back door. Thinking that it was probably something Alex had dropped while working on the dcck, she walked over and picked it up.

She opened it and as she saw the writing in bold red letters she gasped and dropped it on the floor as if it were a poisonous snake.

IT'S PARTY TIME.

Even from where she stood she could see the letters that formed the words. Her heart beat like a pounding drum in her ears, but this time it wasn't terror that shot adrenaline through her. It was a strange form of excitement.

Proof. The note was horrible, but it was definitely proof that the man at the window had been there. He'd been real! It was proof that she wasn't losing her mind after all. He'd been real and the note that he'd delivered was also real.

With trembling fingers she bent down and picked up the note once again. It was impossible to figure out if it was a warning, a promise or somebody's idea of a terrible joke. But it definitely was meant to unnerve her.

Her initial instinct was to call Tom again, but a glance at the clock let her know it was almost midnight. He'd already been here once on what he'd considered a wild-goose chase. She wasn't going to call him away from home for a second time tonight.

She'd contact him first thing in the morning and give him the note. That way he'd know she wasn't going crazy but rather that somebody was messing with her head.

She looked at the note carefully, but there was nothing on it to identify who might be the author. The letters were written in bold by a red marker that could have been bought anywhere and the paper was the ordinary plain white kind sold practically everywhere in town.

She sensed that whatever danger had been here had passed. Apparently the masked man had wanted to deliver his sick promise and with that accomplished he was done…for now.

All she had to do was somehow anticipate what might come next and pray that all of this was just somebody's idea of a sick joke.

Placing the note on the kitchen countertop where she would see it first thing in the morning, she left the kitchen and went into her bedroom.

There was no way she thought sleep would be possible but when she next opened her eyes it was to the sound of hammering in the backyard.

She shot straight up and looked at her clock. After nine. Jeez, she'd slept like the dead. Moments later as she stood beneath a hot shower, she thought of the note and her intention to call Tom.

Funny how a threatening note could make her feel so good, but it was proof positive that she hadn't imagined the man at the window. It was also possible the night that she thought she'd seen a shadow dance across the window it had been the same person peering in at her. Bottom line, it would appear she had some kind of a stalker.

It could be nothing more than a teenager trying to get a peek at her in her underwear. Not all stalkers were dangerous lunatics. It remained to be seen what kind of animal had her in his sights.

Whoever he was, he was a living, breathing human being, and between herself and her brothers they would figure out who he was and why he was doing these things to her. And there would be consequences for his actions.

A smile curved her lips as she walked into the kitchen and saw the men working outside. Although she was still concerned about the note and the vague feeling of threat that had accompanied everything that had happened, she also felt optimistic that the perp would be caught and she could truly get on with her life.

She waved at Alex through the window, her heart beating just a little faster at the sight of him. She'd make coffee and then call Tom.

She glanced at the countertop where she'd put the note the night before—and froze.

It was gone.

Alex wasn't sure when he realized something was wrong with Brittany. She'd waved and smiled at him through the window and then the next time he glanced inside the house she was pulling drawers from the cabinets and dumping them on the floor.

Something was definitely wrong. "Hey, Buck, Gary, go ahead and knock off for the day," he said to his two helpers. "We'll start again first thing in the morning. And don't worry, I'll pay you for the day anyway."

"Cool," Gary said.

As the two young men disappeared around the side of the house, Alex knocked on Brittany's back door. Her brown eyes were wide, glazed with panic as she hurried to the door and unlocked it. She didn't wait to greet him but instead went to another drawer in the cabinet, pulled it out and dumped it on the floor.

"Brittany, what's going on?" he asked.

She fell to her knees and began to sift through the items that now littered the beige tiles. "It's got to be here. I know it's here someplace. I didn't make it up. I swear I didn't dream it." She spoke more to herself than to him as she dug through silverware and hand towels, a sick, frantic energy wafting from her.

"Brittany, what are you looking for?" Alex felt scared, not of her but for her. Her eyes were far too wild and her movements painfully jerky. He got down on the floor next to her.

"It's got to be here. It's got to be here." She didn't look at him as she repeated the words again and again. "It was here last night. It's got to be here now."

He grabbed her hands and her gaze flew up to meet his. Her fingers were cold and trembled as he held them tight. "Talk to me, Brittany. For God's sake what are you doing? What's going on?"

Tears appeared and clung to her long dark lashes while her lips trembled with emotion. "It was a note. A note from him…the man at the window…the man from last night." The words came from her with a jerky rhythm that spoke of her intense stress.

"What are you talking about? Where did you find the note?" Alex asked.

"It was under the back door. I found it after you and Tom left. I thought it was something you'd dropped, but it wasn't. It was a note from him."

"Why didn't you call Tom immediately?"

A flash of annoyance swept over her features. "He'd just been here and he thinks I'm crazy. It was after midnight and I didn't want to call him out again. I put the note on top of the counter and figured I'd call him first thing this morning." A hollow despair filled her eyes. "And now it's gone. It's gone, Alex!"

Once again Alex wasn't sure what he believed, but there was no question that she believed there had been a note and it should be someplace in the kitchen. He looked at the mess she'd made on the floor. There was no note anywhere among the items.

"It isn't here. Let's get everything put back." He began picking up silverware and setting it back in the drawer from where it had come.

For several minutes they worked side by side, neither of them speaking. He could feel the taut tension that rolled off her, but had no way to ease it.

When the drawers were put back in place he led her to the table where she sank down with a weary sigh. Her eyes still held the hollow emptiness of a woman on the edge.

"Don't you see? It was proof. It was proof that I'm not losing my mind, that I'm not suffering some sort of post-traumatic stress that makes me see phantom figures at my window."

"What did the note say?" he asked.

"'It's party time.'" The words trembled from her lips. "I put it right there on the counter before I went to bed." She pointed across the kitchen. "And when I looked for it a little while ago it was gone."

"Is it possible you put the note someplace else and only thought you left it on the counter?" He still didn't know what to believe, but he could tell that she definitely believed what she was telling him.

She leaned back in the chair. "That's why I was checking the drawers. I thought maybe without thinking I'd shoved it in one of them before I went to bed. But it's gone. I know I didn't carry it out of the kitchen. I put it on the counter and now it's gone."

"If that's the case then what do you think might have happened to it?" He kept his voice even and calm in an effort to calm her down.

She leaned forward and her eyes suddenly blazed with life. "I think somebody came in here in the middle of the night and took it." A small burst of laughter escaped her. "God, I really do sound insane, don't I?"

"Maybe a little," he admitted.

She ran a hand across her forehead, as if easing the bang of a headache. "No matter what you think, no matter what Tom and my other brothers believe, I'm not crazy. Somebody is playing games with me." She balled her hands into fists on the top of the table. "This isn't making me crazy, it's starting to really make me mad."

"Did you check the doors and windows to see if

anyone broke in?" he asked. He had no idea if he was playing into some sort of delusion of hers or not, but he desperately wanted to give her the benefit of the doubt.

"I know the back door was still locked this morning. I had to unlock it to let you in."

"What about the front door? The windows?"

"I haven't checked them."

He scooted back his chair. "Then let's do that now."

They went from room to room, checking to see that the house was still locked up tight. The front door was locked and there was no sign of tampering, but in the bathroom in the hallway they found the window unlocked.

"I just can't be sure if it was locked before last night or not," she admitted. "But the screen is still in place."

"The screen could have easily been taken out and put back in again," he replied. "I'm going to go outside and check around the window." As he started out of the bathroom she grabbed his arm.

"You do believe me, don't you, Alex?" Her voice radiated with need.

He hesitated. "I'll be honest with you. I don't know what to believe at this point."

She nodded slowly and released her hold on him. "That's fair," she agreed.

As he went out the front door Alex's head was filled with a thousand thoughts, a hundred emotions. He wanted to believe her. He wanted to believe her because as crazy as it sounded he was already emotionally involved with her.

Emily adored her and Alex was drawn to her like he hadn't been drawn to a woman in a very long time. But he couldn't, he wouldn't bring an unstable woman into his life, into Emily's life.

He'd already been there, done that and had sworn he would never go there again. But he also didn't want to act hastily. He didn't want to distance himself from Brittany if there were any possibility that she might be telling the truth. He'd never thought of himself as a knight in shining armor, but he also didn't want to be a total jerk and just walk away because things weren't going smoothly for her.

He saw nothing around the window to indicate that it might have been tampered with. The grass wasn't trampled down and the dirt didn't hold any footprints. Of course, that didn't mean nobody had been there; it simply meant if somebody had been there they had been extremely careful.

When he returned into the house Brittany was still seated at the table where she'd been when he'd left. His heart squeezed at the sight of her. She had her face in her hands, her shoulders slumped forward in defeat.

She didn't feel as if she could go to her brothers. She'd told him she'd lost her friends after the crime. She was virtually alone with her fears.

She sat up straighter and removed her hands from her face as she heard him come back into the kitchen. "Let me guess, you didn't find anything suspicious."

He sat down next to her. "But that doesn't mean that somebody didn't get inside. Who might have a key to your house?"

She frowned. "All of my brothers have keys."

"But we know none of them would be behind all this. Is there anyone else? An old friend? Somebody you used to date?"

Her eyes narrowed slightly. "Luke Mathis. I was sort of seeing him before I was kidnapped."

"And afterward?" Alex asked, surprised at a small nudge of jealousy that made itself known.

"Luke is a part-time bartender down at Harley's, a bar on the edge of town. He's a good-time kind of guy and after the ordeal I definitely wasn't a good-time kind of woman. We talked a few times on the phone after I was rescued, but that was it."

"Did he have a key?"

"He did, but I can't imagine Luke having anything to do with this," she protested, and then added, "although he does have a wicked sense of humor."

"Can you think of anyone in your life who would do something like this?" he countered. "Maybe somebody you had a run-in with when you were working as a deputy?"

She frowned thoughtfully and once again rubbed her hand across her forehead. "Nobody specific comes to mind. I'll have to think about it."

Once again her shoulders slumped slightly forward. "I can't make sense of any of this." She closed her eyes for a long moment and when she opened them again that steely strength radiated there once again. "All I can tell you is that I know what happened last night. I'm not suffering from delusions. I'm not making things up. I held that note in my hand. I saw the red lettering on the white paper and I saw that man at my window."

There was such a ring of truth in her voice, a certainty shining from her eyes that Alex found it difficult to believe she was a woman suffering some sort of delusional state. "Are you sure you don't want to call your brother and tell him about the note?"

"No, but what I plan to do is go to Harley's and confront Luke. He's always had that kind of a sick sense of humor. Maybe he thinks this is a really funny joke."

"Then the man is an idiot," Alex replied darkly.

For the first time since he'd walked into the house Brittany smiled. "He is kind of an idiot, but he was fun to hang out with for a while." She got up from the table and leaned against the counter. "This isn't your deal, Alex. If I were you I'd run as fast as I could a million miles away from me."

It had only been a little while ago that he'd wondered if that wouldn't be the best thing for him to do. But with the scent of her in his head and her appearing like a tiny speck of an island in a storm-tossed sea, he realized there was no way he intended to walk away from her, at least not right now.

He got up from the table and without saying a word walked over to her and wrapped his arms around her. She leaned into him, as if needing him to anchor her.

Despite the trauma of the morning, despite the questions that plagued his mind, he felt himself responding to her nearness.

She was like an elixir for his blood, a bane to all

the loneliness and heartache that had been a part of his life for so long.

As she raised her face to gaze up at him he knew he was going to kiss her. He had no idea if it was right or wrong. He had no idea if she was right or wrong for him and his daughter. He only knew that at this moment he wanted to kiss her more than anything else he wanted in his life.

Chapter 6

From the moment Brittany had discovered the note gone she'd felt as if she'd flailed around in a sea of madness, a sea that had parted and brought sanity only when Alex's arms had wrapped around her.

She wasn't the kind of woman to depend on a man for anything. She'd always been strong and independent. Even in the face of death she'd remained strong except for one agonizing moment of blackness that she tried never to think about.

But there was no question that at this moment in time she not only wanted, she felt as if she needed Alex to anchor her, to heat the cold places that felt as if they would be icy forever.

When his lips met hers his warmth eddied through her, a welcome sensation she wanted to last forever, and as the kiss deepened she knew it wouldn't be enough. A kiss could never be enough.

She wound her arms around his neck and pressed herself intimately close to him, wanting to lose herself in his heat, in the solid, sweet embrace that promised something more.

And she wanted more. She felt as if she'd been alone for an eternity and right now the idea of being alone for another minute was excruciating.

She wanted, no, needed intimacy. She needed to feel connected with something other than her own doubts, her own fears. She wanted connection with him.

The kiss that she knew he meant to comfort her quickly became hot and greedy as she opened her mouth to his. He'd said he just wanted a friend, but she felt the way he responded to her and in any case at the moment she felt selfish.

For over eight long months she had been utterly alone except for the taunting threats of a madman, followed by the pitying looks from her brothers.

Yes, she wanted to be selfish and take what she needed and damn the consequences. And what she needed right now was Alex, naked with his body tight against hers in her bed.

As the kiss continued she ran her hands up under his shirt, caressing his strong bare back in what she hoped would be an unmistakable gesture of her want. His flesh was smooth and hot.

She felt him tense slightly, but he didn't pull back nor did the kiss end. Instead his hands slid down her back, setting fire to every place they touched until they stopped at the top of her hips.

She wanted him, not as a friend, not as a support system, but as a lover and it was obvious by his arousal pressed against her that he wasn't adverse to the idea.

When the kiss finally ended he stepped back and stared at her, his eyes like flames of electric fire. "I should probably go," he said, his voice slightly husky.

"Alex, I don't want you to go. I want you to make love to me." She took a step closer to him and placed a hand on his chest where his heart beat strong and just a little too fast. "I know you want to, Alex. We can still be friends. It doesn't have to mean anything more than that, but I need you to hold me. I want to feel you naked next to me."

She wouldn't have thought it possible for his eyes to flare any hotter, but they did, but still he took another step back from her as if afraid to take what she freely offered him.

She sensed what he was about to say before he opened his mouth. "Don't tell me I'm not in my right mind," she exclaimed. "Having the deck built was the first thing in eight months I wanted to do for me. Having you is the second."

Her words seemed to snap whatever hesitation in him that might have lingered. In two short strides he had her back in his arms, his mouth hungrily taking hers in a kiss that sent her senses reeling.

All memory of the frantic search for the missing note, the horrid face at the window and every other troubling thought in her head flew from her mind as she gave herself completely to the moment.

It didn't take long for her to tire of kissing in the kitchen. She took him by the hand and led him down the hallway to her bedroom. Her sheets were rumpled as she hadn't made the bed after getting up that morning. It looked ready for two lovers to fall in and rumple further.

"Brittany, I don't want to be part of the craziness in your life," he said as she pulled her T-shirt over her head. "I'm not looking for a wife."

She dropped the shirt to the floor and smiled at him. "That's good, because I'm not looking for a husband. I'm not even looking for tomorrow. I just want here and now with you." She unzipped her jeans and smiled at him. "Are you going to stand there staring at me or are you going to get into my bed and ravish me?"

He grinned back. "Can't I do a little bit of both?"

Within moments they were both undressed except for their underwear. Before she got into bed she opened her dresser drawer and pulled out a condom.

They tumbled together into the sheets that smelled of her favorite perfume and he pulled her tight against him, her bare skin drinking of his.

He was strong and warm and exactly what she wanted, and when his mouth found hers again she found his kiss wonderfully exciting and a testimony to herself that she'd truly survived her ordeal with her life, her very passion still intact.

When the kiss ended he rose up slightly and looked

at her. "I haven't been with anyone since long before my wife died."

"And I've only been with one other man and that feels as if it were a lifetime ago," she replied. Luke had taken her virginity after a night of too much booze and they'd been together twice more after that, but each time had been fast and fairly emotionless and she'd been left feeling as if there should be something more, something better than what she'd experienced.

"I want to go slow," Alex whispered against her ear. "I want to savor every second with you, every inch of you."

She shivered at his words, a promise of sensual pleasure like she'd never experienced before.

His mouth slid down the length of her neck as he tangled his hands in her long hair. She was lost in the width of his back, caressing her hands up and down as the muscles played beneath her fingertips.

She'd wanted him since the minute she'd opened her front door and seen him standing on her porch. She'd wanted him the first time he'd smiled, making his amazing eyes crinkle slightly at the corners and filling her with a welcome heat.

"I've been crazy with wanting you," he said, as if in response to her own thoughts. His lips moved from her throat to her collarbone as she moved her hands up to tangle them in his dark hair.

His chest rubbed erotically against her bare breasts, shooting tingling sensations from her head to her toes. And then his mouth was on her breast, nudging the nipple with his tongue and then suckling with just enough pressure to evoke a moan of pleasure from her.

He'd said he wanted slow and he took it slow. His hands and mouth seemed to touch each and every inch of her until she was gasping with need, crying out his name in a combination of despair and delight.

It didn't take long for their underwear to be disposed of and they pressed the length of their nakedness together, a sensual delight of skin, arousal and fire.

He smelled of a morning shower and spicy cologne, a heady combination that only increased her desire for him. When she wrapped her fingers around the hard length of him he gasped aloud, as if not expecting the intimate touch.

His entire body tensed as she moved her hand up and down the pulsing swell of him. His eyes bored into hers, filled with need that fought for control. "Easy." His voice was a strained whisper and the muscles in his neck were taut. "I don't want to finish before we begin."

With a sudden movement he rolled over to his side, away from her touch, and instead his fingers found her center. Her nerves screamed as he moved his fingers in a slow, circular motion, calling forth a rising tide of sensation that had her trembling uncontrollably.

Then the tide was on her, rushing over her as she cried his name again and again. He rolled away from her and grabbed the condom from the nightstand. Seconds later he eased into her, and she closed her eyes as he filled her up, both body and soul.

He framed her face with his hands and she opened her eyes and gazed at him, and in that moment of eye contact she felt more cherished than she'd ever felt in her life.

A wealth of emotion rose up in her throat. The wonder of life, of this magic moment of complete intimacy, the knowledge that if things had gone bad in that shed with The Professional she would have never experienced this time with Alex. It all rushed over her and tears sprang to her eyes.

He frowned. "Am I hurting you?" he asked worriedly.

She gripped his buttocks and pulled him tighter against her. "No, not at all. You feel wonderful."

He smiled. "You don't know wonderful yet." Then he began to move, sliding his hips back and forth in a slow motion that stole every thought from her head.

Slow and languid soon became faster and more frantic. They clung to each other as she met him thrust for thrust, dizzied by the pleasure that was almost too intense to bear.

When she thought she could stand no more, her orgasm shook through her like an earthquake and she was vaguely conscious of him finding his own release, as well.

They remained locked together, heartbeats finally slowing as she released a sigh of drowsy contentment.

He kissed her forehead, her cheek and the tip of her nose and then slid out of the bed and disappeared into the bathroom. He returned a moment later and slid back beneath the sheet and gathered her into his arms.

She relaxed against him, for the first time in eight months feeling one-hundred-percent safe. Neither of them spoke and she was grateful for the silence that spoke more than any words could say.

She was almost asleep when he stroked a strand of hair away from her face and spoke. "This has been wonderful, but it doesn't solve anything."

With that simple sentence reality slammed back in. Somebody had been at her window. Somebody had given her a note that terrified her with its implication. Was it all just a silly prank or did it imply something more dangerous?

"I know," she finally replied.

"So, what is your next move?" He sat up and reluctantly she did the same. What she wanted to do was stay in bed forever with his arms wrapped around her. But it was time to face her life again.

She worried a hand through her hair. "The first thing I intend to do is call somebody to come over and change the locks on the house."

"Definitely," he agreed.

"I guess my next move will be to go see Luke down at Harley's. He usually works Friday nights so I'll plan on going then."

Alex frowned. "Can't you just call him?"

She shook her head. "I want to ask him if he came into my house last night, if he's the one who tied the balloon to my mailbox and left that note. If I talk to him by phone I won't be able to tell if he's lying to me. If I see him in person I'll know if he's telling me the truth or not."

"I don't want you going to talk to him alone," Alex said firmly. "I'll get Rose to watch Emily Friday night and I'll go with you to Harley's."

She started to protest, but he placed a finger against her lips. "You've already told me you aren't going to your brothers with this. You need somebody on your side, Brittany, and I want to be that man."

He lay back down and pulled her into his arms. Once again they were silent for several long moments and she wondered what he was thinking.

"You ever think about having kids?" he asked.

Of all the things she thought might be on his mind, this definitely wasn't one of them. "Not really," she answered truthfully. "I don't think I'm mother material. Why?"

"You were good with Emily."

"It's easy to be good for ice cream and hair braiding, but that doesn't a mother make."

"She wants a brother or sister. She doesn't understand that I'm not even sure I want to marry again."

"You should marry again. You should find a nice woman who will make an excellent mother for Emily and give her lots of little brothers and sisters, build a family." She ignored the small stab in her heart as she continued. "I have far too much baggage to be the kind of woman you need in your life. You don't want to repeat your past mistake."

This wasn't a conversation she wanted to have. She didn't want there to be any question in his mind about exactly what she had to offer him. "Friends, Alex. That's what we said. It just so happens we're friends who fell into bed together."

"I know. And speaking of Emily, I should probably get out of here. It won't be long till she'll be getting off the school bus."

Once again he slid out of the bed and Brittany looked at the clock on her nightstand in surprise. She was shocked to see how late it was, that they had spent most of the late morning and afternoon in bed.

"I wasn't kidding about Friday night, Brittany," he said as he tugged on his jeans. "You let me know what time you want to go talk to Luke and I'll take you."

"What if I really am just crazy?"

He pulled his shirt on over his head and shrugged with a small smile. "Then I guess eventually we'll figure that out, too." Once again he walked over and kissed her on the forehead. "Why don't you just rest for a little while? I'll lock up as I leave and I'll see you in the morning to work on the deck."

She made no move to get up. The lovemaking had left her boneless and sated, and with the sleepless nights she'd already suffered the idea of a nice long nap seemed infinitely appealing.

At least she'd made it clear to him that she had no interest in being a mommy, that whatever it was they were doing together had no real meaningful future.

He'd surprised her with his talk of children and what was even more surprising was the small whisper of yearning the conversation had stirred inside her.

Maybe someday she'd have a child of her own, when she stopped jumping at shadows and no longer carried with her a terrible sense of dread. She'd think about love and family when she didn't have the ball of anxiety weighing heavy in her heart, when she knew the man who had stood at her kitchen window wasn't a physical threat.

Odd, that nothing had happened before Alex had

appeared in her life. She'd been in the house alone for almost a month and had been feeling better and stronger every day. But the day he'd stepped into her life had been the day the balloon had been tied to her mailbox, the day she thought that everything had begun to go bad.

Who was Alex Crawford? Had there really been a wife who had died of cancer? Had he really been a lawyer in Chicago? Chad had all but admitted that although the two had gone to college together they'd lost touch with each other until Alex had shown up here in town.

It felt almost traitorous to be lying in the bed where they had just made love, wrapped in the sheets that smelled of him, and entertaining these disturbing questions about him.

She rolled over and grabbed her phone from the nightstand and punched in a familiar number. "Hey, Benjamin," she said when her brother answered.

"Hi, dollface. What's going on?"

Of all her brothers, Benjamin was the easiest to talk to. He was soft-spoken, prone to compassion and had a relaxed nature that drew people to him.

"I have a favor to ask you," she said. "But it would have to be a secret just between you and me."

"What do you need?"

"I'd like you to run a thorough background check on somebody." She felt bad even asking, but she had to be sure. She didn't know who to trust right now and as badly as she wanted to trust Alex, she definitely had to be sure about him.

* * *

"How about some lemonade for the hardworking team?" Brittany asked the next day after noon as she carried a tray of drinks out to Alex, Buck and Gary.

"The only thing better than lemonade would be an ice-cold beer," Buck said as he set down his hammer and walked over to the table.

"Sorry, I prefer not to liquor up the men building my deck," she replied.

"Lemonade sounds great," Alex said with a smile as he and Gary joined them.

She poured the drinks from the large pitcher she'd brought and the three men settled into chairs to take a quick break. "It's coming along nicely," she said as she looked at their work.

"Should be finished by the weekend," Alex replied, a sense of pride in his voice as he looked over his work.

"I've always wanted to know what it was like," Buck said, his gaze intently focused on her. "What was it like to be a prisoner of that nut job Larry Norwood?"

Gary elbowed his friend in the ribs. "Jeez, Buck," he muttered beneath his breath.

"What? You know everyone has been wondering. You know you want to know, too. Did he torture you? Use cattle prods and stun guns?" Buck pressed.

"Buck!" Alex said sharply.

"It's all right," Brittany replied. She looked at Buck. "There are much worse things than cattle prods and stun guns. There are much worse things than physical torture."

"He was smart, though, wasn't he?" Buck continued, ignoring Alex's frown of displeasure. "I mean, he
managed to kidnap and kill all those women in Kansas
City and then he almost did the same thing here."

"He wasn't too smart. He's dead and I'm here," she
replied drily.

"That's enough," Alex said. "Back to work."

As Buck and Gary moved away from the table Alex
stepped closer to her. "That was inexcusable," he said.

She shrugged. "Buck's never been known for his
great social skills. He's just curious like I'm sure a lot
of people are."

"If he makes you feel uncomfortable I'll take him
off the job," Alex offered.

"That's not necessary. Besides, the job is almost
done now."

"He's an idiot," Alex said gruffly.

Brittany smiled as she recognized the protective-
ness he apparently felt toward her. "It's fine, really."

"How about dinner tonight?"

She blinked at the abrupt change in topic. She
wanted to have dinner with him. She wanted to go
to bed with him again. She wanted all the things she
shouldn't have, but she hadn't heard back from Benjamin yet and she didn't want things between them to
get any more complicated than they already were.

"I'll have to take a rain check," she replied. "I'm
having dinner with my brother Benjamin and his
wife," she improvised.

"Okay, then maybe Friday before we head to Harley's we can get a bite to eat together."

"We'll see," she replied, refusing to commit to anything at the moment.

As he returned to work with the other two, she carried the pitcher and glasses back into the kitchen. Once she'd rinsed them and stowed them in the dishwasher she returned to the window. Only this time it wasn't Alex who captured her attention. It was Buck.

There had been a glee in his eyes as he'd asked her the questions, a faint glint of admiration in his voice as he'd spoken of The Professional.

How could anyone admire a killer? She didn't understand how, but she knew it happened. Some of the most notorious serial killers received thousands of love letters a year from women and notes of admiration from men.

Buck had little in his life to admire. His parents had been alcoholics who had virtually been unavailable to him from the time of his birth. He'd been kicked around by most people in town and had few friends. Was it any wonder he'd find an inappropriate man to look up to?

Was it possible he'd tied the balloon to her mailbox? Wore the ski mask and stood at her window? Was he a threat or playing some immature silly game?

She turned away from the window and picked up her phone and punched in her sister-in-law Edie's phone number. "I was wondering if I could invite myself to dinner tonight," she said after the initial greetings.

"Absolutely," Edie replied. "In fact you're in luck, Poppy and Margaret are coming over and doing the cooking so you know whatever it is will be good."

They arranged for the time and then hung up. Poppy was actually Edie's grandfather, Walt Tolliver. During the time that Brittany had been held captive by The Professional, Walt had become something of a small-town hero when he'd helped break a case of grave robbing and illegal dumping.

During the same time he'd fallen in love with Margaret, the older woman who had been housekeeper for the Grayson family for years. The two hadn't married, but liked to tell everyone they were living in sin and loving it.

They were a fun couple, each proclaiming to be the best cook and bickering good-naturedly about cooking styles. At least it would be an entertaining night and Brittany wouldn't feel as if she had lied to Alex about her dinner plans.

Still, later that afternoon as she got ready to head to Benjamin and Edie's, her thoughts weren't on Alex, but back on Buck and the excitement that had lit his eyes as he'd questioned her about her time with The Professional.

Chapter 7

Antonio's Italian Restaurant was the closest thing to fine dining in the small town of Black Rock and it was where Alex took Brittany on Friday night for dinner.

As the hostess led them to a small round table in the back of the dimly lit establishment, Alex couldn't keep his eyes off Brittany.

She wore a little black dress that hugged every curve and skimmed the tops of her thighs. Strappy black high heels accented the shapeliness of her long legs. Her hair was pulled up in a ponytail, exposing the long, slender column of her neck and allowing gold-and-black earrings to dangle freely.

He still wasn't sure what he believed about her and her phantom stalker. There had been no more drama for the past couple of days. The deck was officially finished except for a few finishing touches and tonight after dinner they'd confront Luke Mathis to see just how sick his sense of humor was.

But right now Alex didn't want to think about what came before or what would come after this moment. Brittany was stunning and at least for the length of the meal she belonged to him alone.

He knew he shouldn't think of her that way, but since the afternoon of their lovemaking he'd had trouble thinking of her any other way. There was a part of him that recognized that heartache might be ahead, but he wasn't sure he was completely capable of guarding his heart where she was concerned.

As they made their way to the table he was aware of the other diners watching Brittany and he could tell she was aware of them by the rigid straightness of her back.

She only relaxed when she slid into her seat, which faced away from the rest of the diners. "Feel like you just walked the plank?" he asked teasingly.

"Actually, it wasn't as bad as I expected," she replied, although she reached for her glass of water as if her throat had gone too dry.

"I keep telling you the more people see you out and around the less interesting you'll be."

She grinned. "That kind of makes it sound like the more of me you get, the more bored you are."

He laughed. "You know I didn't mean it that way," he protested.

"I know." She picked up the oversize menu. "I'm starving."

"Good, I like a woman with an appetite."

"I'm definitely not one of those women who peck on rabbit food and call it dinner. In fact, I happen to know that the lasagna here is fabulous."

"That's good to know since this is my first time here," he replied.

"You really should bring Emily here some night. They make car-shaped pasta for the boys and little purse-shaped pasta for the girls."

"That sounds fun. Maybe the three of us could come back some evening."

She lowered the menu and looked at him seriously. "What are we doing, Alex?"

He shrugged. "We're having dinner before we go to Harley's so you can talk to Luke," he replied, deliberately being obtuse.

She set the menu aside and frowned at him. "You know that's not what I mean."

He frowned for a long moment. "I don't know what we're doing. I only know that I don't want it to stop," he said truthfully.

Her cheeks flushed with a hint of color. "You know this isn't going anywhere, that we aren't going anywhere."

"Friends," he said, and then he couldn't help but add with a smile, "with occasional benefits."

"You shouldn't be wasting your time with me."

"I'll let you know when I think you're a waste of my time," he replied easily.

At that moment the waitress arrived with her order pad and a basket of warm bread and butter. They placed their orders and then she departed, leaving them alone with the slightly uncomfortable conversation they'd been having before she'd arrived.

"I just don't want anyone to get hurt," Brittany said. "Be honest with me, Alex. You aren't sure what to believe about my phantoms and my notes and whatever. Do you really want somebody around Emily who isn't cut out to be a mother? A woman who might be losing her mind?"

"You're right, I'm not sure what to believe about the things you believe have happened, but I know that you're kind and funny and caring, and why wouldn't I want Emily to be around a woman like you? I told you before, Brittany, I'm not sure I'm in the market for marriage again, but life is too short not to connect in meaningful ways with people you care about, and I care about you."

It was a long speech and when he was finished he sat back in his chair and waited for her reply. "I just don't want anyone to get hurt," she finally repeated.

"Right now the only thing I'm anticipating might hurt me is that I'll burn the roof of my mouth on the lasagna. Now, drink your wine and tell me about this Harley place we're going after dinner."

Dinner conversation remained light and pleasant and just as she'd predicted the food was delicious. They lingered over dessert and coffee, knowing that the best time to hit the tavern was later in the evening.

"I have a confession to make," she said and something in her tone of voice caused his stomach muscles to cramp.

"What kind of a confession?" he asked.

"I had my brother Benjamin do a background check on you."

Alex sat back in his seat in surprise. "You did?"

"I had to be sure that you were who you said you were," she replied, her voice holding an unspoken apology.

"And what did he find out?"

A small smile curved her lips. "That you really are who you say you are." The smile faltered. "I'm sorry, Alex, but I had to be sure."

"No need to apologize. I don't have any deep, dark secrets and I understand your need to be sure." And he did. She'd needed to assure herself that he was worthy of her trust, and after all she'd been through there was no way he could blame her for that. The stories he'd told her about his life could have been nothing but fabrications with the intent to get closer to her, especially if he had nefarious intent toward her.

"Did you go to Harley's often?" he asked, changing the subject.

"Too often," she admitted. "Especially after I started seeing Luke. I worked hard during the day as a deputy, but I played even harder at night." She shook her head and picked up her wineglass for a drink. "It's amazing how being close to death can change your priorities, transform your life."

"So, not much of a party girl anymore?" he asked lightly.

"Not at all. Life is too short to waste it partying with people who don't bring meaning to your life." She stared down into her wineglass and when she finally looked back at him her eyes were impossibly dark and equally impossible to read.

"Larry Norwood had set up a shed with five tiny cells. For almost three months I was alone in one of those cells. You can do a lot of thinking in three months. For the first week I refused to eat what little he'd bring out to me. I spent my time exploring the cell, looking for some sort of escape route, but there was no way out."

He wanted to stop her, didn't want her to relive the experience here and now, but he also didn't want to interrupt her if she needed to talk about what she'd endured.

"After that first week I started to eat everything he brought to me, knowing I'd need to keep up my strength if I were going to try to somehow escape. I woke up every morning hoping that one of my brothers would burst in and save me and I went to bed every night with a sense of despair I've never known before."

He reached across the table and took one of her hands in his. "You don't have to do this, Brittany. I don't have to know any of it."

She nodded and tightened her fingers around his. "But I want you to. I want you to understand." She leaned forward, her eyes flittering in the semidarkness of the restaurant. "The silence was terrible, but the worst part was when I'd hear him whistling right before he entered the shed. I never knew if he was bringing food or coming in to kill me or coming for one of his chats."

"His chats?"

Again she nodded and her eyes took on the glaze of somebody remembering unpleasant things. "He'd come in and pull up a chair in front of my cell and then he'd talk about all the things he intended to do to me when he finally had all his cells filled with women." Her fingers chilled beneath his. "Terrible things. Things that wouldn't kill me, but would cause excruciating pain. He never touched me in any way, but there are nights I have nightmares about the things he promised to do to me."

"Why was he waiting until he got the other women?" Alex asked in an effort to understand exactly what she'd faced.

"His real thrill came in having an audience. He wanted to torture and kill us each one at a time while the others watched. Of course initially I didn't understand that, so each time he came into the shed I thought I was going to die."

The glaze in her eyes lifted. "I can't put into words what that feels like, how it eats away at your very soul. It changes you. It changes who you are at your very core." She pulled her hand from his and leaned back. "My brothers don't get it. They don't realize how much I've changed and that's why I have trouble talking to them. They think a new pair of shoes or a fancy purse is going to make me feel better because that's what I used to love."

"I didn't know you before, Brittany. So I can only

tell you that I like the woman you are now, that to me you represent a strength of character that I admire."

Her eyes darkened once again. "I'm not as strong as you think I am. I'm not as strong as anyone believes I am."

She averted her gaze from his and for a moment he thought he saw a whisper of secrets and realized there was probably more that she wasn't ready to tell.

She released a small, embarrassed laugh. "Sorry, I didn't mean to get into all that now."

"It's okay. I told you anytime, anyplace if you need to talk, I'm here for you."

She smiled. "But you probably didn't intend for a conversation like this to take place in the middle of dinner at Antonio's Restaurant."

He returned her smile. "This is as good a place as any." He sobered. "Brittany, let's just take things slowly. Because that's all we really have—one day at a time."

She released a sigh that sounded like relief. "I just don't want to lead you on in any way."

"I'm a big boy. Don't you worry about me. Don't you worry about anything but finishing that dessert and then getting your key back and maybe some answers from Luke."

The conversation returned to more normal topics, the beautiful weather, the flowers she intended to plant around her new deck and the party she planned to throw when everything was perfect in her backyard.

"Of course you and Emily will be invited," she said and then finished the last of her wine. "And my family and I'm thinking about inviting some of my old girl-friends."

He raised an eyebrow. "The ones who made you uncomfortable after your rescue?"

She frowned and toyed with one of her dangling earrings, making him want to take it off and nibble on her earlobe. "I've been thinking about that. I think maybe in those first weeks after my rescue I pretty much pushed everyone away, including some well-meaning friends. I felt safe at Benjamin and Edie's and I was afraid that anyone else might pull me out of that feeling of safety, so I protected myself by with-drawing. I miss having girlfriends to do lunch or just chat on the phone."

She offered him a beautiful smile and dropped her hand to her lap. "I think I'm finally really healing and it's in large part thanks to you."

"To me?" He looked at her in surprise.

"You and Emily got me out of my house for ice cream. You have me here now. You've made me re-alize I can continue my life here in Black Rock, a normal life after everything that happened to me."

She might not recognize her own strength, but she obviously had no idea the core of character that ex-isted in her. And there was no question that he was as drawn to the woman she was inside as he was drawn to her physical attractiveness.

One day at a time, he reminded himself as they left the restaurant. She'd made it clear that she wasn't mother material and he couldn't seriously contemplate a relationship with a woman who wasn't.

There was no way this thing with her could have a happy, romantic ending, but he'd meant what he'd said to her. He didn't know what they were doing, but he wasn't ready to stop.

Two things surprised Brittany. The first was that she'd had a sudden desire to talk to Alex about her time with The Professional. Although she hadn't told him everything, she'd been surprised by the cathartic relief she'd felt in telling him what she had.

The second thing that surprised her was the bad case of nerves tightening her stomach as they pulled up in front of Harley's. This was the most public place she'd been since her kidnapping and rescue.

The parking lot was clogged with cars and trucks, attesting to the fact that it was a busy Friday night. Inside would be people she hadn't seen since her kidnapping.

She glanced over to Alex as he steered into a parking place. He was his usual hot self tonight in a pair of black slacks and a short-sleeved white dress shirt. She'd found the familiar scent of his cologne oddly comforting all night long and she'd found his attentiveness to her throughout the meal more than a little bit sexy.

Still, as she looked at the tavern doubts once again roared through her. What if it hadn't been Luke who had come into her house? What if there hadn't been anyone at the window? What if that note had only been a figment of her imagination?

She was feeling healthier, more ready to face the

rest of her life with each day that passed, but no matter how much rational thought she had in her head she couldn't rid herself of a nebulous feeling of dread that somehow the bad things weren't behind her but rather were racing toward her with the speed and power of a locomotive.

Maybe it would all be dispelled now, if she found out that Luke was behind everything, believing he was being funny or trying to get her attention in an inappropriate way.

As they got out of Alex's car she tried to still the nervous flutter in her tummy. Even from the parking lot the sound of the band could be heard, the bass of the drum vibrating in the air, like her heart thundering in her chest.

"Sounds like a happening place," Alex said as he took her arm in his.

"That's because it's the only place in town where you can drink and dance and get a little crazy. And I'll warn you, people do get a little crazy in there."

"Consider me duly warned. And maybe before the night is over I can steal a dance from you."

"You like to dance?" she asked curiously.

"I used to, although Linda didn't like to. She was always afraid she'd slip and fall and hit her head or break a bone."

She tightened her grip on his arm, wondering just how much he'd sacrificed by loving his wife. "Before this night is over, we'll definitely dance," she promised.

Inside Harley's it was dark, smoky and loud. The

band on the stage was a local one, not great but adequate for public consumption. But it wasn't the dimness or the smoke or the noise that overwhelmed her—it was the amount of people who immediately flocked to her.

Friends and acquaintances crowded around her as if she were a visiting rock star. She hugged closer to Alex's side as he maneuvered her toward the bar in the back of the place.

She began to relax as she realized everyone wanted to give her a hug, pat her on the back and tell her how great it was to see her out and around again. There were no awkward questions, only support coming at her in waves.

She smiled as she heard a familiar squeal and a tall blonde came rushing at her. Brittany released her hold on Alex's arm as she was smothered in a tight hug and a fog of familiar perfume.

"OMG," Melissa Winters exclaimed as she stepped back from Brittany. "It's about time you joined the land of the living."

Brittany grinned and at that moment realized how much she'd missed Melissa, who had been one of her very best friends before she had been kidnapped.

Melissa slid her gaze to Alex and then looked back at Brittany. "And when you join the land of the living you definitely do it right!" She held out a hand to Alex. "Melissa Winters, dispatcher at the sheriff's office and former partner in crime with Brittany."

"Alex Crawford, neighbor and friend," Alex replied.

"God, I hope you're more than a friend. She deserves only the best," Melissa exclaimed, making Brittany's cheeks flame with color.

"Why don't you let me buy you both a drink?" Melissa offered.

"Thanks, but I'm just here to speak briefly to Luke. Why don't we try to plan to meet for lunch this week?"

"You mean it? I'd love it, Brittany." Melissa gave her another hug and then went back to the dance floor where her date awaited her.

Brittany looked forward to lunch with Melissa. There had been a time when she and the tall blonde had been nearly inseparable. Melissa had been one of the people who had tried to be there for her after her rescue, but Brittany had pushed her away and instead wrapped herself in a cocoon of isolation.

"You okay?" Alex breathed in her ear.

She smiled and nodded. "Better than okay." It was just as Alex had told her—after the initial flurry of greetings everyone drifted away, leaving her and Alex to continue to make their way to the bar.

The moment she saw Luke she wondered what had ever drawn her to him in the first place. Although he was tall and slender he might have been good-looking without the mop of shaggy brown hair and the growth of whiskers that managed to make him appear unkempt rather than cool. His ears were pierced and a large tattoo of a skull covered one side of his neck.

He'd been her bad-boy rebellion, a choice to make her brothers crazy in an effort to declare herself grown and independent. He was nothing like what she'd choose for herself for anything meaningful or lasting. Luke had simply been a good time for a little while and nothing more.

Still, his features lit up at the sight of her and at the same time she was aware of Alex stepping backward, giving her the opportunity to greet Luke alone.

Luke stepped out around the bar and grabbed her hands in his. "Jeez, you look great, Brittany. I'm so glad to see you."

"Thanks, I'm feeling good about things."

"Man, I've missed you like crazy." He reached one of his hands up as if to caress her face, but she took a step back so his hand fell to his side. His green eyes narrowed as if with a touch of displeasure.

He shoved his hands into his jeans pockets and continued to gaze at her. "So, what's up? I thought I'd hear from you before now. I haven't stopped thinking about you. When I saw you I thought maybe you came in to see me, you know, to kind of pick up where we left off before everything happened."

"Actually, I came in to see you, but I need to ask for my house key back. Luke, we had some fun, but things have changed over the past four months for me. I'm sorry." Even though she'd already changed all the locks on her house, she wanted to see his reaction when she asked for her key back.

"Nothing changed for me, Brit. I've just been waiting for you to come around again, you know, giving you the space I figured you needed after what you'd been through."

As if she really believed he'd just been sitting around waiting for her for the past four months. "I'm sorry, Luke. Like I said, things have changed. I've changed."

"I just thought maybe by now you'd be ready for a few laughs...some good times," he said.

"You were always good for that," she agreed, wondering if his idea of a few good laughs was to scare the hell out of her. "By the way, did you come by my place the other night? Maybe use your key to come inside?"

It was impossible to read his features, but he shook his head negatively. "Now, why would I do something like that?" he countered.

"I don't know, maybe to play a joke of some kind." She desperately wanted it to be him. She needed him to be the explanation for what had happened. A sick joke. A warped sense of humor. A balloon, a break-in and a stupid note—she could accept and forgive that. She just wanted some answers that made sense.

"I don't know what you're talking about. But I see you have a new boyfriend." He gestured toward Alex. "Who is that joker?"

"He's a friend," she replied.

"Yeah, well, I've got to get back to work." He pulled his key ring from his pocket, yanked off the key she'd requested and slid it across the bar. "Have a nice life, Brittany." He didn't wait for her to reply but turned and went back behind the bar.

"You think he did it?" Alex asked as he walked up beside her.

"Hard to tell." She frowned and looked back at Luke, who was flirting with a young blonde at the bar.

"He told me no, but he also said he was kind of waiting around for me to start up our relationship again. He didn't seem too happy when I told him that wasn't going to happen."

"You want to get out of here?" he asked, obviously concerned that she might be upset.

She smiled, refusing to allow Luke's petulance or the fact that she hadn't really gotten an answer from him to ruin her evening. "Not before we have that dance we talked about."

At that moment the band began to play a ballad. "With pleasure," Alex said and led her to the dance floor where he took her into his arms.

Despite the fact that she'd reminded him only an hour before that they would be, could be nothing more than friends, his arms around her felt like home.

That scared her. The Professional had taken her innocence and dignity from her. But she had a feeling if she wasn't careful Alex would take her heart.

Chapter 8

A knock on the door sounded just after ten on Saturday. Brittany had just gotten out of bed, after having lingered for a long time thinking about the night before and dancing with Alex.

She opened the door and was surprised to see Emily clutching a stuffed pink bear in her arms. "Can I come in?" the little girl asked and without waiting for an invitation swept past Brittany and into the living room where she plopped down on the sofa with a frown.

Brittany closed the door and followed, wondering what was going on. "I don't want to be a bother. I just need a minute away from Mr. Poophead Daddy," Emily exclaimed.

Brittany bit back a smile. Ah, trouble in parenting paradise. "I was just about to fix me an English muffin with some jelly. Would you like to join me?"

"That would be lovely," replied the child who had just called her father a poophead.

She followed Brittany into the kitchen, set her bear in one chair and sat in the chair next to the stuffed animal while Brittany pulled out the package of muffins. "Does your daddy know where you are?"

"I told him I was running away and never, ever coming back again." Emily lifted her chin as if in a show of defiance.

"I see you brought a friend with you."

Emily nodded. "This is Lady Bear. She's my bestest friend in the whole wide world."

"She's a lovely bear. Maybe we should call your daddy and let him know where you and Lady Bear are so he won't worry too much," Brittany suggested as she put the muffins in the toaster.

At that moment the phone rang. Brittany was unsurprised to hear Alex's voice when she answered. "I know this sounds crazy, but is Emily there?"

"She is. We're just about to sit down to eat a muffin and jelly," Brittany replied.

"Tell Mr. Poophead I don't want to talk to him," Emily said.

"She doesn't want to talk to you right now," Brittany said into the phone.

"She called me a poophead, didn't she?" Alex heaved a deep sigh. "I'm sorry she's bothering you with this. I'll come down and get her."

"No, it's okay. She needs some time. I'll walk her home after we've had a little girl talk."

He hesitated. "Are you sure? This definitely isn't your problem."

"I'm positive and our muffins just popped up from the toaster, so I'll see you later." Brittany hung up the phone and then slathered the muffins with butter and grape jelly. "Milk or juice?" she asked.

"Milk, please."

Once the drinks and muffins were on the table Brittany sat next to Emily. "Want to talk about it?"

Emily took a bite of her muffin, leaving a smear of grape jelly on her cheek. Brittany picked up her napkin, leaned forward and swiped it off. Emily smiled gratefully and then her smile fell.

"Megan has a birthday party this afternoon and Daddy said I could go. I already got her a present and wrapped it in really pretty pink-and-purple paper and now he says he has a meeting and can't take me. Megan is one of my bestest friends in school and I have to go to her party or else her feelings will be hurt." Her lower lip puffed out a bit. "Daddy is such a poophead."

"Can't your grandma take you to the party?" Brittany asked.

Emily took a swallow of her milk, leaving a milk mustache on her upper lip, and then shook her head. "She has a woman meeting about something. Mr. Poophead said I have to go with him to his meeting and be a good girl 'cause it is about a big job for him. So, I runned away. Can I have another muffin?"

Brittany got up to fix the muffin and her mind whirled. *Don't get involved,* a little voice whispered in her head. *It's just a ride to a party,* another voice replied. *What else do you have to do with your afternoon?*

"What's Megan's last name?" she asked as she placed the second muffin in front of Emily.

"Megan Jefferson, and I bought her a really cool pink purse with sequins and she's one of my very best friends and she'll be so sad if I can't come to her party." Emily was on a tangent, repeating herself in her frustration. "You go to a friend's party, that's what you're supposed to do. It's like a rule for little girls."

Brittany knew the Jefferson family. She'd been friendly with Megan's mother, who worked at the bank. "Maybe I could take you to your party." The words were out of Brittany's mouth before she'd realized they'd formed in her brain.

"Really? You could do that?" Emily jumped out of her chair and threw her arms around Brittany's neck. "That would be so wonderful." Her kiss on Brittany's cheek was sweet and slightly sticky from the jelly.

Brittany laughed. "Why don't you finish up your muffin and then we'll talk to Mr. Poophead to make sure it's okay with him?"

Minutes later they walked down the sidewalk to Alex's house. As Emily chattered about the party, Brittany thought about the night before. She and Alex had shared not one dance, but three before leaving Harley's. She hadn't gotten the answers she'd sought from Luke, but the night out had been yet one more step in her re-emergence into life.

When they'd reached her house once again she'd

known that Alex wouldn't have minded if she'd invite him in for another bout of lovemaking, but she'd kissed him on the cheek and thanked him for the night.

She desperately wanted to make love to him again and that's why she wasn't going to let it happen. Her heart was getting too involved and she had to make decisions now that were best for both of them.

Taking Emily to a birthday party as a favor was one thing; feeling the warmth of Alex's arms around her, the strength of his naked body against hers was quite another.

She would never again be the deputy she'd once thought herself to be and she would never be the woman Alex and Emily needed in their lives.

Alex greeted them at the door, his brow furrowed with concern as he looked first at his daughter then at Brittany. "I'm so sorry," he began.

Brittany held up a hand to halt his apology. "Emily tells me she has a birthday party to attend this afternoon and you and Rose aren't available to take her."

"I'm meeting a guy this afternoon who wants his basement remodeled. Today was the only time he had to meet with me," Alex explained. "It's a big job and I tried to explain to Emily that sometimes business has to come first."

"I have an alternative plan," Brittany said.

"She said if it's okay with you she'll take me to Megan's party," Emily exclaimed. "Tell her it's okay, Daddy. Please, please!"

"Daddy? What happened to Mr. Poophead?" Alex asked with a raised dark eyebrow and a wry grin.

Emily sidled up next to him and gave him a sweet smile. "I was just upset, Daddy. I didn't really think you were Mr. Poophead."

Alex rolled his eyes and Brittany stifled a giggle. "I really don't mind taking her to the party," Brittany said. "I have nothing going on this afternoon."

"I'd hate to impose," Alex said.

"As if I haven't imposed on you before," Brittany replied drily.

"If you're sure…" he responded.

"Oh, she's sure," Emily said. "And it was all her idea, not mine." She clapped her hands together with excitement.

"That's true," Brittany agreed. "Now, all I need to know is what time."

"The party is from two to four. My appointment is at two-thirty and I'm not sure how long it will take me," Alex replied.

"Why don't I take her to the party and then bring her back to my place and you can get her there when you're finished?" Brittany asked.

"That sounds like a plan." Emily beamed at both of them.

"Then I'll be here at around a quarter till two and we'll go from there." Brittany smiled at Emily. "I know how important birthday parties are."

"I knew you'd understand." Emily gave her a smile that bordered on hero worship. "Girls understand these things."

"Why don't you take Lady Bear upstairs and make sure your present is all ready to take?" Alex suggested.

"Okay. See you later, Brittany." On light little feet she raced up the stairs and disappeared.

When she was gone Alex turned back to face Brittany. "I think perhaps my daughter is a little bit of a manipulator."

"Goes with the female genes," Brittany said with a smile. "Really, it's okay. I know the Jefferson family and it's not a big deal."

"It's a big deal to Emily, so I thank you."

When he smiled at her like that she wanted to fall into his arms. Instead she murmured a goodbye and stepped out the door. She'd been vastly relieved when Benjamin had called to let her know that Alex Crawford was exactly what he'd told her he was—a former attorney who had lost his wife. There had been no red flags in his background. The man didn't even have a speeding ticket on his record.

He was the kind of man she might have wanted in her life forever, if she were a different kind of woman. At least nothing had happened in the past couple of days to scare her. But unfortunately, nothing had happened in the same few days to clear up the mystery of the man at her window and the disappearing note.

She felt as if she were in a curious state of limbo, not quite willing to trust her own mind yet refusing to admit that she was losing it.

As she entered her house she shoved all these thoughts to the back of her mind. All she needed to think about for the afternoon was getting a little girl to a birthday party.

At one forty-five when Brittany pulled up in Alex's driveway Emily danced out the door. She had Lady Bear in one arm and a pretty pink-and-purple wrapped package in the other. Alex followed after her and as Emily got into the backseat he walked around to the driver window.

"Thanks again," he said. "I should be home by the time the party is over."

"I'll just take her back to my house and you can call when you're home," Brittany replied.

Within minutes they were on their way to the Jeffersons'. "I'm so excited. I love birthday parties and this is the first one I've been to since we moved here," Emily said. "Do you like birthday parties?"

"It's been a long time since I've been to one," Brittany replied. She hoped there were no red balloons to remind her of anything bad.

"There's cake and ice cream and games," Emily continued. "When is your birthday?"

"In less than two months," Brittany replied.

"Maybe I could have a party for you. We could have a big cake and chocolate ice cream, and you and me and Daddy could play party games. You could be queen for the day."

Brittany flashed a quick smile at Emily as she pulled into the Jeffersons' driveway. "We'll see." She had no idea how things would be in two months' time, but she had a feeling she and Emily and Alex wouldn't be having a birthday party together.

She parked the car and then turned to the little girl. "Maybe it would be best if we let Lady Bear stay here in the car," she suggested. Brittany remembered that little girls could be cruel and Emily showing up clutching her favorite stuffed animal might set her up for some jabs.

Emily frowned thoughtfully. "Maybe you're right," she conceded.

"Why don't we put her in the backseat? We'll buckle her in with the seat belt so she'll be safe and sound."

"That sounds like a plan," Emily replied with what Brittany had discerned was her favorite phrase.

They buckled the bear in and then walked to the front door.

Mary Jefferson greeted Brittany with a smile of delight. "It's so good to see you," she exclaimed as she opened the front door. "I've missed seeing you at the bank."

"Thanks, it's good to see you, too. I just came by to drop off Emily Crawford for Megan's party."

"Oh, please join us, unless you have someplace else to go." Mary smiled conspiratorially. "To be honest, I wouldn't be adverse to adult company to kind of even the odds. You know, the two of us against thirteen squealing, giggling six-year-old girls."

Emily smiled and grabbed Brittany's hand. "It's okay. You can stay. It's gonna be fun."

"Sure, I'd be glad to help out," Brittany agreed.

By the time they'd walked through the neat living room, the sound of the party drifted in from the backyard. When Mary opened the back door Emily dropped Brittany's hand and ran toward her friends, who were gathered in a tight-knit circle and seemed to be doing a group squeal.

Mary motioned Brittany into a chair at an umbrella table nearby. "I figure I'll give them about thirty minutes to work off some energy and then do some organized games and the cake and ice-cream thing. How about a glass of iced tea or something?"

"No, thanks. I'm fine."

"You look great. I've thought about you often over the past couple of months," Mary said.

"It's taken me a couple of months to get back on my feet and feel good about getting out and around," Brittany replied. She tensed, waiting for the uncomfortable questions to come.

"Well, it's good to see it finally happening." She then began chatting about the joys of parenting a six-year-old, the challenges of birthday parties and how happy she was to have an adult to talk to while the party took place.

Brittany found herself relaxing and realized she'd done her town a disservice in not embracing the support so many of the people had offered her after her ordeal.

She gave herself to the joy of participating in the party atmosphere, and there was such joy. As she laughed with the girls at silly antics and watched Megan's delight as she opened her presents, she found a happiness she didn't know was possible.

As she ate ice cream and cake next to Emily, she

enjoyed the girlish chatter about school activities and Justin Bieber's hair and pink shoes with sparkly heels.

There was an innocence here that soothed her, a shining promise for the future among these children who had the possibility of all things good gleaming from their eyes.

Was this why people had children? Because they filled the world with laughter and believed in Easter bunnies and Santa Claus? Was it because it was impossible to be in a bad mood when a little girl giggled or gave you an impulsive hug?

"Do you miss your mommy?" Emily asked when the party was over and they were back in the car driving to Brittany's house.

"Yes, sometimes I do." Brittany slid her gaze sideways to the little girl. "Do you miss yours?"

Emily frowned thoughtfully. "I mostly don't remember mine. Daddy tells me stuff about her sometimes, but I don't really remember her by myself much at all. But I had such fun at the party. Did you have fun?"

"I did," Brittany agreed as she pulled into her driveway.

"You looked funny when you played Pin the Tail on the Donkey." Emily giggled. "You pinned the tail on his nose!"

Brittany laughed. "I guess I need a little more practice." She parked the car and saw Alex sitting on her stoop. "Oh, look, your daddy is here."

Emily jumped out of the car carrying a big purple balloon and a handful of party favors and ran toward her dad, who stood as Brittany opened her car door. Brittany tried to still the leap of her heart at the sight of him.

Drat that man with his white T-shirt, worn jeans and the tool belt that hung low around his sexy lean hips. Why did he have to make her heart beat so fast? Why did the mere sight of him have to make her want to leap into his arms?

"Daddy, we had so much fun and I got a balloon and some candy and a paper purse that I can color any color I want. I'm going to make it pink with yellow stripes. Don't you think that will be pretty?"

"I think that will be beautiful," he agreed and his gaze shifted from Emily to Brittany.

"Did you get the job?" she asked.

"I did." A sense of pride deepened his voice. "It's a full basement remodel and should keep me busy through most of the summer."

"That's good."

"I guess I'll get the kid home and try to unwind her from all the sugar I'm sure she had at the party."

Brittany smiled. "Good luck with that. I think I have a little sugar crash in my future, too."

"Emily, tell Brittany thanks for taking you," he instructed.

Emily wrapped her arms around Brittany's waist and hugged her tight. "Thank you, thank you!"

Brittany leaned down to return the hug. Just before Emily released her she took her hand and lightly caressed Brittany's cheek. Her green eyes sparkled with determination. "I know I'll never, ever forget you in my whole life."

And then she and Alex were walking away and Brittany stared after them, tears burning in her eyes. She'd been so afraid that Alex might steal her heart but already his daughter had torn off a huge chunk that she had a feeling she'd never get back.

It was almost ten and Alex sat on the sofa, Emily sprawled next to him sleeping. She'd begged him to let her stay up late since it was Saturday night so they'd decided to watch a movie. It wasn't long after the intro credits had rolled that she'd fallen asleep.

He should have moved her to her own bed an hour ago, but instead he'd remained next to her, just enjoying the sweet bubble-bath scent of her.

Getting the remodeling job had only confirmed to him that he was where he belonged, doing what he was supposed to do. With the real-estate market in the tank, many homeowners were opting for remodeling rather than selling their homes and he had a feeling that once word got out that he was good and dependable he'd have more work than he knew what to do with.

He'd consciously willed himself not to think about Brittany all day, but it had been difficult. Thoughts of her struck him at the craziest times.

As he'd slipped into his shoes that morning he'd remembered how badly he'd wanted to take hers off after they'd gotten back to her place from Harley's.

Those sexy strappy black heels had made him half-insane.

He'd not only wanted to take off her shoes, but also slide that sexy black dress from her body and carry her to her room where they would make love until dawn. But that hadn't happened. She'd shut him down with a quick good-night kiss on her doorstep.

He would be finishing up her deck Monday and maybe then it would be easier to gain some distance from her. And he needed distance. He was definitely getting too close, wanting more of her than she'd indicated she wanted to give back to him.

Friends with benefits was fine as long as nobody's heart got involved, but his heart was already pretty far gone.

He rubbed Emily's back, deciding it was time to get her into bed. When she didn't stir he rose and then scooped her up in his arms.

Her legs wrapped monkey-style around his waist and her head rested on his shoulder and his love for her roared like a lion inside him.

She needed a mom who could take her shopping and talk about girl stuff. She needed a mom who could hold her when she cried and tell her everything was going to be okay.

Alex worked at being the best father he could be, but in his heart he knew it could never be enough, that little girls needed mommies to be completely well-adjusted.

And Brittany didn't want to be a mom, didn't believe she had what it took to be a mom. How selfish was it of him to stay involved with a woman who had already told him she would never be anything meaningful in his life…in Emily's life?

Emily's room was an explosion of pink. Pink bedspread and curtains, throw pillows and lamp, it was a room for a princess. His little princess. Still holding her in his arms, he pulled down the spread and placed her on the bed.

Sleepily she opened her eyes and smiled at him, a sweet smile that shot through Alex's heart, his very soul. The moment was fleeting and then a tiny frown danced across her forehead. "Where's Lady Bear?"

Uh-oh. A sinking feeling overwhelmed Alex as he realized he hadn't seen the beloved pink bear all evening. "You stay right here. I'll go downstairs and see if I can find her."

He left her bedside, hoping he could easily find the stuffed animal, or if he didn't, that she would have fallen back asleep by the time he returned to her room and they could do a full search in the morning.

He did a cursory search downstairs without the bear showing up and then climbed the stairs once again, hoping this wasn't going to be a big deal.

Emily hadn't fallen back asleep; rather she was sitting up in the bed, a look of wild panic in her eyes. "Did you find her, Daddy?"

"I didn't, but I'm sure we'll find her in the morning," he replied.

"No! I need her now. You know I sleep with Lady Bear every night." Tears welled up in her eyes, breaking Alex's heart. He knew how important that bear was to her.

"When was the last time you had Lady Bear?" he asked, knowing that there was no way Emily would go back to sleep without that bear in her arms.

Emily's frown deepened as tears trekked down her cheeks. "I took her to the party."

Alex groaned inwardly. It was already after ten; he wasn't eager to call the Jefferson home to find out if a pink bear might have been left there.

"But I didn't take Lady Bear into the party," Emily said. She swiped at her tears. "She's in Brittany's car. We buckled her into the backseat before we went into the party. That's where she is!"

"I'll tell you what, I'll call Grandma and see if she can come up and sit with you for a few minutes so that I can go to Brittany's and get Lady Bear."

Emily threw her arms around him. "Oh, thank you, Daddy. You're the best in the whole wide world."

"You stay here in bed. I'll be right back." Alex left Emily's room and went into his own. Thankfully he knew that Rose wasn't an early-to-bed kind of woman. He was sure she wouldn't mind coming down for a few minutes while he retrieved the beloved bear.

Within fifteen minutes he was opening his front door to allow Rose inside. She'd driven down since it was after dark and she greeted him with a smile of humor. "There's nothing so dire as a missing Lady Bear at bedtime."

"You've got that right," he agreed. "At least we know where Lady Bear is and it should only take me five minutes to get it, but I didn't want to leave her here alone while I ran down to Brittany's and I also didn't want to get her out of bed and all revved up again."

"Go, get the bear and in the meantime I'll go sit with Emily and tell her a story. Maybe I can get her back to sleep before you come back home. My bedtime stories are usually boring enough to put anyone to sleep."

"Without her bear, good luck with that," he said drily.

He stepped out into the warm night air and wondered if perhaps he should have called Brittany to let her know he was coming. But he had a feeling she wasn't an early-to-bed kind of person, either, and it was only a few minutes after ten.

It was a perfect night, the moon almost full overhead and the scent of dewy grass and flowers hanging in the air. Alex walked leisurely, enjoying the sound of crickets chirping and the relative hush of a small town at night.

In Chicago at this time of night there would have been the rush of traffic, sirens blowing and bus brakes squeaking. The city had been a cacophony of noise he definitely didn't miss.

As he approached Brittany's house he saw a light shining dimly from some room in the back of the house. Good, she was still awake. Her car was parked in the driveway and by the light of the moon he could see Lady Bear in the backseat, appearing to give him a gleeful smile.

He was about to head to the front door when something caught his attention…a shadow…a faint noise… he wasn't sure what, but something drew him around the side of the house.

Noise. It was definitely a faint noise that didn't belong in the stillness of the night. Maybe somebody was trying to steal some of the lumber that was still back there. He rounded the corner to the back of the house and froze.

A figure stood at one of the back windows. The man obviously didn't see Alex as he worked to remove the screen from the window. He was clad in black jeans, a black T-shirt and wore a ski mask over his face.

Brittany's phantom. The words thundered in Alex's head. He wasn't a figment of her imagination. He was as real as the sudden rapid heartbeat in Alex's chest.

He must have made a noise…something that alerted the man of his presence. For a split second Alex saw the glittering eyes beneath the mask and then the man whirled and ran in the opposite direction.

Alex took off after him. There was no way he wanted the man to get away. The man jumped the chain-link fence that surrounded Brittany's next-door neighbor's backyard and Alex followed, easily clearing the fence without trouble.

His only thought was to catch the man, to find out who he was behind his mask, who was tormenting Brittany. What had been his intention in trying to take off the screen? To get inside? To harm her in some way?

Alex was in good physical shape but apparently so was the man he chased, who sprinted over the other side of the fence and continued to run.

By the time Alex had chased him for three blocks his heart felt as if it might explode in his chest and the only sound he could hear was his own gasping breaths. Still he pushed on, keeping the man in his sights as he tried to gain ground.

Desperation drove him, burning in his chest as they continued to race. As the masked man turned a corner, Alex pushed harder, faster but by the time he turned the same corner the man was gone.

Alex halted, eyeing the darkness before him as he tried to catch his breath. He had no idea in what direction the man had run, no way to know how to catch him. He'd disappeared, as if the very night had swallowed him whole.

For several minutes Alex remained stock-still, watching the darkness all around, trying to get a sense of where he might have gone, but it was no use.

With a sense of failure, he turned and headed back to Brittany's house. His chest ached from his exertion, as did his leg muscles, but he was eager to get to her, to tell her that she wasn't going crazy.

Then it suddenly struck him and he didn't know what was worse—the fact that she wasn't losing her mind or the knowledge that somebody was really after her.

The Real Professional, that was how he liked to think of himself. He leaned against the side of a house to catch his breath. Adrenaline flushed through him, pumping blood through his veins with a power that made him feel more alive than he'd ever felt in his life.

It had almost happened. He'd almost gotten to her. He'd almost gotten caught. He wasn't sure which made his heart pound faster.

When he knew that his pursuer was gone, he left the side of the house and hurried to his truck parked along the curb in the distance.

He'd almost made it happen...the beginning of a new reign of terror for Black Rock. He'd read and researched everything he'd been able to find about Larry Norwood and his crimes, crimes that had been left incomplete in Black Rock.

He intended to re-create those crimes and make sure they were done right. He was going to kidnap five women and then kill them slowly, one at a time.

He'd worked for the past month in a shed on the back of an abandoned property and now everything was ready for the party he'd throw, a party that would have the entire town talking about The Real Professional instead of The Professional, who hadn't managed to finish what he'd started.

People would tremble in their beds at night. They would respect his cunning, his cleverness and his evil.

Sliding into his truck, he tamped down both the excitement and the tinge of disappointment that threatened to consume him. It was all supposed to have started tonight, but unfortunately his plans had been ruined.

No problem, he told himself as he started the

engine. There was always tomorrow. He placed the syringe and Taser in the glove box. It was amazing what you could buy on the internet. The Taser would have incapacitated her long enough for him to inject her with the drug that would have knocked her unconscious and lasted until he could take her to the special place he'd built.

Of course, he couldn't completely replicate The Professional's crime. Most of the original victims who had escaped had now left town and were no longer available to meet the fate they should have before.

But one thing was certain. It all had to begin with Brittany.

She had been the first taken in the original crime and she would be the first in his crimes. It was just a matter of time, but she was marked to attend the "party" that had never happened. He was The Real Professional, better and smarter than the original, and the town of Black Rock would talk about him long after he'd moved on.

Chapter 9

The rapid knock on her front door tore Brittany from her sofa with a startled gasp. She was clad only in a pair of soft black cotton shorty pajamas with tiny pink hearts all over them. She cursed the fact that her robe was in the bedroom and wondered who was at her door at this time of the night.

The knock came again. "Brittany, it's me."

She hurried to the door at the sound of Alex's voice. When she unlocked it and opened it, he flew in, his eyes wild and his breathing rapid.

"What's wrong?" she asked, immediately feeling the urgency wafting from him.

He flashed her a tight smile. "I need your phone and I found your sanity."

She pointed to the phone on her end table. "What do you mean you found my sanity?"

He walked over to the phone, picked up the receiver and quickly dialed. "Rose, this is going to take longer than I expected. She's asleep? Good. I'll be home as soon as I can."

"Where did you find my sanity?" Brittany asked again when he'd hung up. She felt as if she were going to scream if he didn't explain himself immediately.

"At your back window where I saw a man in a ski mask trying to remove your screen. Call your brother."

"You saw him?" Brittany remained frozen in place, her heart beginning a rumbling rhythm.

"I not only saw him, I chased him for almost five blocks before I lost him in the darkness. Now, call Tom. He was real and he was trying to get into your house."

She wasn't going crazy! There had been a man in a ski mask at her window, a note left behind. Somehow, someway The Professional was back and she wasn't losing her mind.

She dialed Tom's number. "You need to come here right away," she said when he answered. "Somebody tried to break into my house and I'm not going crazy. Alex caught him midact and tried to catch him but he got away."

She hung up and looked at Alex. "He's on his way." She had no idea if he reached for her or she reached for him, but suddenly she was in his arms, his heart beating as fast as her own.

"I'm not crazy," she said into the front of his T-shirt.

"No, you aren't," he replied softly.

"Somebody is really after me."

He tightened his arms around her and hesitated a moment. "Yes, apparently somebody is after you."

She raised her head and looked up at him. "Why?"

"I don't know, but we're going to find out."

She remained in Alex's arms until Tom arrived. He wasn't alone. Brittany's brothers Benjamin and Caleb were with him.

"What were you doing here?" Tom asked Alex, who had sat on the sofa next to Brittany as her brother began to ask him questions. Caleb and Benjamin had gone outside to look at the window.

Brittany looked at Alex. She hadn't thought to ask him what had brought him to her house. "Lady Bear," he said to her and then looked at Tom. "My daughter's favorite stuffed animal is in Brittany's car. We didn't realize it until I tried to put Emily to bed so I came down here to retrieve it and that's when I heard a noise and followed it around to the back of the house and saw the man at Brittany's back window."

"What did he look like?" Tom had out a small notepad and pen and was poised to take notes.

"Black T-shirt, black jeans and a ski mask." Alex fought the impulse to reach over and take one of Brittany's hands in his.

"He left me a note," Brittany said.

Tom frowned. "A note?"

"The last time I called you about seeing him. After

you left I found it. It said, 'It's party time.'" She explained about deciding to wait until morning to call Tom and then that the note had disappeared.

"Why didn't you call me back that night?" Tom asked with exasperation.

Brittany lifted her chin and glared at her brother. "Because that night you thought the man was a figment of my imagination. You thought I'd be fine with a little therapy."

Tom looked chagrined. "Okay, let's concentrate on the here and now." He looked at Alex once again. "Anything else you can tell me about the man you saw?"

"Shorter than me, slender and fast as hell," Alex replied. "I chased him for four or five blocks and then lost sight of him at the corner of Elm and Apple Lane."

"The red balloon tied to my mailbox, the ski mask and the note, it's just like before," Brittany said, fighting against the shiver that tried to creep up her spine. "I know Larry Norwood is dead. But I think this is some sort of a copycat."

"Maybe it's just a kid trying to freak you out," Tom replied.

"It's more than that," Benjamin said as he and Caleb came into the living room. "He was definitely trying to get inside. The screen was cut and half-off and the window is cracked just above the lock. I'd guess another couple of minutes and he would have been inside."

"And why would he want to get inside?" Brittany asked, but nobody replied.

"Benjamin and I are going to head out," Caleb said. "We'll check out the neighborhood, see if we find anything or see anyone."

Tom nodded and looked at Brittany. "And you're coming home with me tonight. I don't want you here alone until we can get a full security system installed."

She started to protest, not wanting to leave her home, but she also didn't want to be stupid. There was nothing to say that the man wouldn't return later that night. "All right," she agreed. "I'll go pack a suitcase and first thing tomorrow morning I'll make arrangements for a security system to be installed."

She looked at Alex. Her instinct was to run into his arms once again, to feel his warmth, the security of his strong embrace. "My car keys are on the kitchen counter if you want to get Lady Bear." The best thing she could do for Alex and Emily was distance herself from them.

Somebody was after her and she had no idea how dangerous he might be. There was no way she wanted Alex or Emily tangled up in this mess.

As Alex left to go into the kitchen to get her keys and retrieve the bear, Brittany turned back to her brother. "I want my gun back," she said.

He frowned. "That gun was yours because you were my deputy. Are you ready to come back to duty?"

She wanted to. She desperately wanted that part of her life back, but she couldn't forget that dark moment in the shed with The Professional. She truly believed she wasn't fit for duty and it broke her heart.

"No," she finally said, her voice a mere whisper.

Tom studied her for a long moment. "Go pack your bag. We'll sort things out later."

She was in her bedroom throwing things into a small suitcase when Alex came into the room. He placed his hands on her shoulders and gazed at her somberly. "Are you okay?"

"I hate leaving my house, I hate what is happening, but yeah, I guess I'm okay," she replied.

He stroked a light caress down her cheek with the tips of his fingers. "At least I'll know you're okay with your brother."

She forced a smile. "I'll be fine. Go home, Alex. Take Lady Bear and I'll talk to you later."

Within minutes Alex was gone and Brittany was putting her suitcase in the back of Tom's patrol car. Caleb and Benjamin were still canvassing the area but Brittany had little hope that they would find anything useful.

"Just what we need, a copycat," Tom said in disgust as he pointed the car toward the house where he, his wife, Peyton, and little Lilly lived.

"Are there any other missing women in town?" Brittany asked.

"None that have been reported." His jawline was tense, as was his grip on the steering wheel. "As if Larry Norwood weren't enough now we have to have some wannabe running around town."

"Running around me," Brittany replied darkly.

Tom shot her a quick glance. "I'm sorry I didn't believe you the first time. The balloon...the man at the window—I dismissed your concerns and for that I'm really sorry."

She reached out and placed a hand on his arm. "Apology accepted." She dropped her hand and leaned back in her seat. "To be honest I was beginning to think I was losing my mind."

"You should have told me about the note."

She shrugged. "When it disappeared I didn't figure there was any point in telling you. I thought you'd just write it off as some delusion I was suffering."

"But that means somebody was in your house."

She nodded. "I know. I changed my locks the next day and Friday night Alex and I went to Harley's to talk to Luke to ask him if maybe he'd been inside my house playing one of his stupid jokes. Of course he denied it."

"Maybe it's time I have a talk with Luke," Tom replied as he pulled into his driveway.

Brittany released a sigh. "I can't imagine Luke having anything to do with this. It's not a joke, Tom. If this truly is a copycat, then he'd be trying to replicate the original crime." A wave of horror swept over her as the full realization struck her.

"I was the first one taken in the original crime. If he's repeating everything, then I'll be the first woman kidnapped again this time around."

The sense of dread that had been with her for so long now roared inside her because she knew if she had to go through it all again, this time she wouldn't survive.

* * *

"I won't be chased out of my house," Brittany told Tom the next morning. She'd slept surprisingly well in Tom and Peyton's spare bedroom considering the events of the night before.

She'd gone to bed afraid and had awakened angry. She'd lost almost eight months of living her life and enjoying her home to The Professional. Four of those months she'd been locked in a cell in a shed. She wasn't going to lose another day of her life because of him. "Besides, we can't know for sure that this is a copycat at work. It still could be just some kid having fun at my expense."

"Brittany, you have to be reasonable," Tom began.

"I am being reasonable," she exclaimed. "I've already called Bob Lockheart. He's going to meet me at the house in an hour to install a state-of-the-art security system and you're going to give me back my service revolver until this is all over."

"Of course he is," Peyton said firmly as she grabbed her husband's arm. "And if he doesn't then I have my own handgun that I'll be more than happy to loan to you."

Tom looked at his wife and then back at Brittany. "What, is this some sort of a female conspiracy? Brittany, this isn't a game."

"You're right," she replied sharply. "It's my life and I'm tired of hiding from it." She drew a deep breath and released it slowly. "Tom, I'm not being stupid or irresponsible. With a security system and a weapon, nobody is going to be able to get me. I want to be in my house. I need to be in my house, living my life. If I can't do that then I might as well have died at the hands of Larry Norwood," she ended in frustration.

Tom ran a hand down his face, the gesture doing nothing to erase the lines of worry. "We almost lost you once, Brittany. I just don't want to make any mistakes here." His voice was filled with an emotion she rarely heard. She stepped toward him and he embraced her in a tight hug.

"You're a good sheriff, Tom," she said when he released her. "And Benjamin, Caleb and Jacob are good deputies. You'll figure this out and in the meantime I'll make sure I stay as safe as possible."

Half an hour later she was headed back to her house with her gun stuffed in her waistband and, if she were to admit it to herself, a little bit of fear riding in her heart.

The easy way out would have been to stay with Tom and Peyton or any of her other brothers and their wives, but that would have simply made her a prisoner all over again.

She had absolutely no idea who she couldn't trust, but she knew with certainty who she could—her brothers and Alex. Those were the only men she'd allow close to her until this whole ordeal was over.

There was no way to know if it was somebody trying to replicate the original crimes. There simply wasn't enough evidence to support the theory, but she had to function with the possibility that it might be.

As she pulled into her driveway she was surprised

to see Jacob sitting on her front porch. He was another victim of The Professional, but in a different way.

As an FBI agent working in Kansas City, Jacob had hunted Larry Norwood when he'd kidnapped five women in that city. Larry had even had phone contact with him, taunting calls that had made Jacob an intimate participant of the crime. Unfortunately, Larry had managed to complete his "party" in Kansas City and Jacob had been left to pick up the pieces, to see the victims in death.

The result had been that he'd quit the FBI and moved into a cabin on the Graysons' family property where he lived like a hermit until Norwood began his games in Black Rock.

"Don't you have anything better to do than hang around here?" she asked as she carried her suitcase up the walk to the porch.

"Figured I'd hang out until Lockheart arrives to install that security system." He took the suitcase from her. "I see you're armed." He nodded toward the gun at her waist.

"And dangerous," she added as she unlocked her front door. He followed her in and set the suitcase in the foyer. "How about some coffee? I can have a pot made in a jiffy."

"Sounds good," he agreed. He locked the door behind him and then followed her through the living room and into the kitchen.

"Sure you want to be here, Brittany?"

"No place else I'd rather be." She pulled the coffee can from the cabinet and set about getting it brewing as he sank down into a chair at the table and watched her.

"Got any ideas?" he asked once the scent of the fresh brew began to fill the air.

"Not really." She sank into the chair opposite him. "I told Tom he might want to check out Luke Mathis down at Harley's. Luke and I were hanging out before I got kidnapped and he had a key to the house before I changed the locks, but I really don't think he's behind all this." She frowned thoughtfully. "I don't know, you might want to talk to Buck Harmon."

"Why Buck?"

"He's been helping Alex on the deck and he's just said some things that make me think he's pretty fascinated with The Professional."

"Half the people in town are fairly fascinated with The Professional," Jacob replied as she got up to get their coffee. "Face it, aberrant behavior is intriguing to most people."

"But most people don't set out to emulate somebody like Norwood," she replied.

Jacob took a cup from her and smiled. "It would be nice if everyone in the world knew how to play nice with others, but if that were the case the Grayson family wouldn't have jobs. And speaking of jobs, when are you coming back to yours?"

Brittany stared down into her coffee cup. As always when she thought of her job she was taken back to that desperate moment in time when she'd realized she'd never be a deputy again.

"Talk to me, Brittany," Jacob said softly. "There

has to be a reason why you've avoided coming back to work. We've both experienced the darkness of The Professional. There's nothing you can say to me that will surprise or horrify me."

Brittany knew that if she were going to talk about it with anyone, it would be Jacob, who had seen the faces of the dead women Larry had left in his wake.

Suddenly she wanted to talk, she wanted to tell him about that moment when she'd lost all sense of herself. "You know what he was capable of, Jacob," she said, her gaze once again on the coffee in her cup. "Every day he'd sit and tell me how many ways he was going to hurt me, how long it would take him before he'd finally kill me."

She felt a swell of emotion fill her chest. "I tried not to listen, tried not to think, not to imagine what he was saying to me, but day after day his words started to seep into my head, into my very soul."

Jacob said nothing, as if knowing that no words he offered could make this any easier for her. He simply sat completely still, his gaze intent on her.

"For the first week I spent every waking moment trying to find a way out, looking for any weakness I could exploit to escape, but there was none. By the time a month had passed he'd gotten into my head, Jacob." The words clogged in her throat as she tried to continue despite the clump of guilt and shame that rose up in the back of her mouth.

She raised her coffee cup and took a sip, trying to swallow around the lump. Jacob remained patient, not blinking an eyelid as he waited for her. Carefully she set the cup back on the table. "There was one night when he left me alone that my fear spiraled completely out of control."

She stared at her brother, remembering that moment of despair that she'd never, ever felt before in her life and hoped to never feel again. "I wanted to die, Jacob." The words were a mere whisper. "I wanted to die on my own terms, not on his. I wanted to commit suicide."

Her words hung in the air, stark and ugly, and yet with them came the release of a pressure she hadn't realized she possessed.

Jacob took a sip of his coffee and leaned back in the chair. "The only difference between you and me is that you looked for a way to end your pain immediately and I holed up in the cabin and tried to end my pain by drinking myself to death and cutting myself off from any human contact. That doesn't make us bad lawmen, Brittany. It makes us human."

She stared at him. She wasn't sure what she had expected, but acceptance and understanding hadn't been it. A bit more of the pressure in her chest released.

"Brittany, a lawman who doesn't know fear is a dangerous one, one who I would never want to work with. Fear is the way your body tells you that you're in danger. And that moment when you wanted to take your own life and not let him take it, don't fool yourself—if that's what you'd really wanted, you would have found a way. You're a survivor, Brittany, and instead of feeling guilty or ashamed about that time, you should celebrate the fact that you got through it."

Brittany thought it was the longest speech she'd ever heard Jacob say and she knew deep in her heart that he was right. Had she had a moment of weakness? Of wishing she would die before Larry Norwood could torture her to death? Absolutely. But it had only lasted very briefly and then she'd gotten on with the act of survival.

Just then Bob Lockheart arrived to install the security system. Jacob hung around for another hour and then left after Brittany insisted she'd be okay by herself. By two that afternoon she was alone in a house that had the security of a castle.

Her talk with Jacob had given her a peace she hadn't had since her rescue. She'd felt such shame about giving up all hope, such despair that she'd known such weakness. But she also knew the situation she'd found herself in had been one that few people would ever experience. And Jacob was right. She had survived. With the weight of self-loathing out of her heart, her thoughts turned to Alex.

She'd scarcely had time to talk to him last night before Tom had whisked her away. She eyed the phone. What she wanted more than anything was to hear the sound of his voice, to be in his arms, and that was exactly why she wasn't going to call him.

There was somebody after her, a man who might be trying to copy the original crimes of The Professional. At the moment her world was an unsafe place and the last thing she wanted was to bring Alex or his daughter into that world.

She knew it all had to come to an end, that their relationship was going nowhere. As much as she adored Emily she wasn't in a place to take on the role of motherhood.

Friends with benefits, that's all it was supposed to be, and now it was time to end even that. He'd be over first thing in the morning to finish up the last of the details on her deck and ultimately that's all she'd wanted from him, that's all she could accept from him.

Chapter 10

Alex had thought about Brittany all night on Saturday and most of the day Sunday. He'd hoped to hear from her during that time but when he didn't he figured she was probably busy with her brothers.

He hadn't meant to fall in love with anyone. He especially hadn't meant to fall in love with her, but Monday morning as he left his house it was love for her that accompanied him.

He'd fallen in love with her and he wanted to build a life with her. She'd said she wasn't the motherly type, but every interaction she'd had with Emily had shown him otherwise.

She was not only beautiful and bright, she was also kind and loving, and that's all she needed to be his wife and a stepmother for Emily.

It was crazy that he'd only known her a little over a week and yet knew so clearly what was in his heart for her. Besides, how long was love supposed to take? Was there a time requirement for the heart to become involved with somebody? No, love had nothing to do with time and everything to do with emotion. And his emotions screamed that he was in love with Brittany Grayson.

When he arrived at her house Gary and Buck were already there. As Alex finished up the last of the woodwork, they were going to do a general cleanup of the yard, picking up scraps of lumber and whatever needed to be done.

"Hey, boss," Buck greeted him. Gary smiled and raised a hand. "We were just wondering if you planned on using us on your next job."

Alex glanced toward the back window, hoping to get a glimpse of Brittany but the window was empty and there was no sign of her.

"Sure, I could use your help. It's going to be a big remodel job that's probably going to run us into the end of summer."

"Cool," Gary said. "My folks will be happy to still see me working."

"You've both been good help," Alex replied. "And now, let's all get to work." Once again he looked at the back window, but there continued to be no sign of Brittany.

Maybe she'd stayed on at her brother's house, he thought as he got busy. It was about noon when he realized she was home. He spied her inside and waved.

What he wanted to do was ask her if she was okay, if any of her brothers had managed to figure out who had tried to break into her house. He wanted to hold her in his arms and assure himself that she was really all right.

The fact that she didn't come outside to say hello concerned him a bit, but he stayed focused on finishing up the last of the work.

By two o'clock he'd sent Gary and Buck home. The work was done, the yard was clean and there was nothing left to do. He knocked on the back door and she appeared. It took her a minute before she got the door open.

He couldn't help the smile that stretched his lips at the sight of her, the very scent of her that wafted in the air. She was dressed in a pair of jeans and a bright yellow T-shirt that enhanced the darkness of her hair, the beauty of her eyes.

When had she become his heart? When had she broken down every barrier he'd ever tried to erect against marrying again?

"We're finished," he said as she gestured him into the house. Once he was inside she keyed in several numbers on a pad next to the back door.

"New security," she said. "Anyone tries to open a door or a window an alarm rings not only through the air, but also directly into the sheriff's office."

"Good idea. How are you doing?" He sensed a distance in her, a distance that created a hard knot of tension in the pit of his stomach. He noticed the gun sitting on the kitchen table. "Looks like you're ready for anything that might come your way."

"Whoever this creep is, we think maybe he wants to re-create the original crime, and that means if he sticks to the script I'll be the first one he attempts to kidnap."

"That's what you think the man was trying to do two nights ago?"

"I can't imagine why else he would have been trying to get into the house."

"Is this the way it happened last time? He took you from here?" The mere thought of what she'd already been through moved him forward a step toward her.

"No, he took me from my car. He was hiding on the floor in the backseat and before I knew he was there he'd slapped a hand across my mouth and stuck a needle in my arm that almost instantly made me unconscious. Whoever this new guy is, it's obvious he's trying to emulate The Professional, and that means I'm probably top on his hit list."

He so wanted to pull her into his arms, to somehow make this right. He wished he had the capacity to find the bad man and put him behind bars where he could never hurt or frighten Brittany again.

But as he took yet another step toward her she stepped back and grabbed her purse. "I'll just write you the check for the balance of what I owe you." She fumbled in her purse and pulled out her checkbook.

She was definitely distant and he was surprised to realize that it scared him, that the hard knot in his chest had grown in size. "How about we have dinner together tonight to celebrate me finishing up the deck?" he suggested.

"I don't think so." She finished with the check and ripped it from the pad, then held it out to him, her dark eyes shuttered so that it was impossible for him to guess what she might be thinking.

He took the check, folded it and stuffed it in his pocket. "Then what about tomorrow night?" He was aware he was pushing it, but he needed to know where he stood, where they stood. "Or the night after that… or the night after that?"

She worked a hand through her hair, as if to unknot an invisible tangle. It was a gesture he'd come to recognize as nerves.

"Alex, my life is complicated right now. I think it's best if we are just neighbors and nothing more."

"But I'm falling in love with you." He hadn't meant to say the words. They'd just spilled from his lips as if unable to stay contained another moment.

For the first time since he'd walked into her kitchen her facade cracked and he saw genuine pain flash in her eyes. "That wasn't part of our deal. I'm not in a place to love or be loved. I told you I certainly wasn't ready to be a mother. We need to stop this, Alex, before either one of us gets in any deeper."

"But I don't want to stop and I'm already in deep. I want you in my life, Brittany. You're everything I ever wanted in a woman."

"I'm not right in your life right now," she exclaimed, the pain still sharp in her gaze. "I'm not even right in my own life right now."

She sat at the table, her gaze not meeting his. "I'm not so different from your wife, Alex. You see me as being strong and in control, but you don't know that I wake up in the middle of the night afraid to draw a breath, afraid to get out of bed and see what might be hiding in the shadows."

"When that happens I can wrap my arms around you and let you know you're safe. You are strong, Brittany. You're nothing like Linda was before her death. And what you and I were building together was something wonderful. Don't throw it all away now."

He could tell his words hadn't broken through to her. Her eyes were once again dark and emotionless. "Does this have something to do with the man who's after you? Are you trying to protect me and Emily?"

She sighed in obvious frustration. "I'm trying to protect you and Emily from me," she exclaimed. "I'm not right for you or for her, and you and I pretending to do the friends-with-benefits thing while doing otherwise is foolish. You're a nice man, Alex. Find a nice woman and build a life for yourself and your daughter."

There was a finality in her words that brooked no further discussion, no reason for him to continue the conversation except for the aching numbness in his heart.

"You'll let me know if there's anything you find with the deck that needs further attention?" he asked stiffly.

"I will."

"And you'll let me know if there's anything, anything on this earth that I can do for you?" His voice held the hollow ring of a man with a breaking heart.

"Goodbye, Alex. And thanks for everything."

He stood for a long moment, memorizing every strand of her shining hair, every facial feature that had brought him such joy. She looked toward the back door, as if wishing him through it. And at that moment he made her wish come true and left.

Brittany buried her face in her hands, fighting against the tears that threatened to fall. It had been harder than she'd expected. She hadn't realized just how deeply Alex and Emily had dug themselves into her heart until now, with the gaping wound of their absence burning in her chest.

She was in love with Alex, and she adored Emily. But she was selfish and flighty. She wasn't the woman Alex believed her to be. She wasn't cut out to be a mother to a needy little girl.

And if that weren't enough, she was now a virtual prisoner in her home, waiting for a madman to make his next move, praying that a new "party" wasn't in her future.

It was her love for Alex that had forced her to push him away, and even if Tom or one of her other brothers managed to get the man after her in jail tomorrow, nothing would change where things stood between them.

It was over. It was finished. She'd had hours of lovemaking with him, a week of the warmth of his arms and the beauty of his smiles. It had to be enough, because she'd never be enough for him and his daughter.

She pulled herself out of the kitchen chair, needing to do something, anything to take her mind off the ache of loss, the despair of what might have been that resonated through her.

She wandered through the house like a lost soul. She should be ecstatic that the deck she'd dreamed about was finished. But she couldn't have a family barbecue anytime soon, not knowing who she might be placing in danger by inviting them to her home.

Pausing in the doorway to her bedroom, the ache in her heart intensified as she remembered that afternoon with Alex in her bed. He'd been a wonderful lover, on every physical and emotional level.

And she'd never know that wonder again. She'd never see him gaze deep into her eyes again with a look that made her feel as if she were the most important person on the face of the earth.

No man had ever made her feel the way Alex had. They'd both been fools, playing with emotions they couldn't control. She moved away from the bedroom and decided to work on her laptop. She should work on Alex's website, but she had no idea where they now stood on that particular project. Maybe a couple of hours of cybersurfing would make her forget that she'd just shoved the man she loved out of her life.

She spent most of the afternoon and early evening on the computer, lost in the minutia of other people's lives. As she read posts her mind worked to try to come up with a suspect.

Larry Norwood, despite being the town vet and a married man with two children, had been a secretive man. He didn't have friends, didn't hang out with male buddies who might have made it onto a suspect list now. There was no indication whatsoever that he had worked with a partner.

She still wasn't sure what to think about Luke. The few phone conversations she'd had with him immediately following her rescue had been awkward, but he hadn't said anything that would make her believe he identified with Larry Norwood in any way.

So, who? Who would want to emulate a serial killer? Somebody powerless, somebody who felt disenfranchised by the town? Certainly Buck fit that description.

She eyed the gun on the table. She'd carried it from room to room with her throughout the afternoon, not letting it out of her sight. Security was all well and good, but there was nothing like a bullet to stop a bad man.

Her phone rang several times during the course of the evening. Each of her brothers called to check in on her. When she spoke to Tom, she told him that when this was all over she would be ready to return to her job as a deputy. He was pleased with her decision and when she hung up the phone after speaking with him she realized if nothing else good came out of this experience, at least she'd regained the dignity, the confidence that Larry Norwood had almost stolen from her.

She'd been a darned good deputy and she'd still be

a good one. She'd almost allowed Larry to take that from her, but Jacob was right, she was only human and that didn't make her less of a good deputy.

It was just after eight when the phone rang again. She steeled herself as she recognized Alex's number on the caller ID. She thought about not answering, but avoidance really wasn't her style.

"Brittany, I'm sorry to bother you but I have a huge favor to ask you." His voice was filled with urgency. "I just got a call from Rose. She thinks she's having a heart attack. I told her to call an ambulance, but I'd like to get to the hospital as quickly as possible and I'd rather Emily not be there with me."

"Of course you can bring her here," Brittany answered without hesitation. She knew Alex wasn't the type to play games. This was real and it was life-and-death and she could definitely understand him not wanting his daughter there.

"I'll be right there." He hung up before she could reply. She hurried to the front door and quickly disarmed the security system, then, remembering the gun on her kitchen table, she ran back into the kitchen to put the weapon in a safer place.

As she picked up the gun, she glanced around the kitchen, trying to figure out where a curious six-year-old wouldn't find it. She finally tucked it into the upper cabinet next to the sink.

"Emily?" she called as she thought she heard somebody at the door. She hurried back through the living room to see headlights in her driveway and Emily getting out of Alex's passenger door.

She clutched Lady Bear in one arm as she raced toward the house. Alex leaned his head out the driver window. "I don't know how long I'll be," he yelled.

"Whenever," Brittany replied as Emily came through the door. They both waved to Alex as he tore out of the driveway, then Brittany reset the security and led the little girl into the living room.

"My grandma is sick," Emily said as she sat on the sofa and hugged her bear close to her chest.

Brittany sat next to her. "I know, but hopefully the doctors can fix her right up and she'll be back home before you know it."

"I hope so." Emily's lower lip trembled.

Brittany pulled her close against her, knowing what Emily needed more than anything at the moment was a hug from a real person, not the hug from a stuffed bear.

For several long moments Emily clung to her as Brittany smoothed her silky blond hair and murmured meaningless nothings that oddly enough seemed to help ease some of Emily's fears.

She finally sat up and swiped at her cheeks. "I hope you don't think I need to go to bed or something like that."

"Actually, what I was thinking was maybe I'd paint your fingernails and then you could paint mine."

"Now, that sounds like a plan," Emily said in obvious delight.

"You sit tight and I'll go get the polish," Brittany said. She got up from the sofa and went into the adjoining bathroom off her bedroom. Beneath the sink cabinet she had dozens of different colors of polish. The desire to polish her fingernails to match her outfits had fled at the same time her desire for high heels and purses had gone, resigned to a place of unimportance in the new life she was building.

Still, she was glad she had all the polish when she carried it into the living room and Emily squealed with excitement. Emily chose a pretty pink to be painted on her nails and while Brittany worked the little girl kept up a running chatter of everything in her world.

School, boys and ruminations on life in general— Emily shared her opinions about it all with an openness that Brittany found charming.

When they were finished with Emily's nails, it was her turn to paint Brittany's and she decided she wanted to do each nail a different color.

Brittany sat patiently as Emily carefully chose each color and painted each nail. By the time she was finished Brittany had a kaleidoscope of colors and more than a little bit of polish outside her nails.

"My daddy was sad this afternoon," she said suddenly as Brittany waved her hands in the air to dry the polish.

"Did he tell you why he was sad?" Brittany asked cautiously. Surely Alex wouldn't share with his daughter any details of the scene earlier in her kitchen.

"He just said it was a blue kind of a day. That's what we call it when we're sad. I guess it was a blue kind of a day when my mommy died and it's gonna be a blue day if my grandma doesn't get better."

"It's definitely not a blue kind of day for me," a familiar deep voice said. Gary Cox walked into the living room with that goofy, friendly smile on his face and a Taser in his hand.

"Gary?" For a long moment Brittany couldn't process his presence here in her house. She stared at him blankly, trying to make sense of it.

Someplace in the back of her mind she recognized she'd made a mistake…a terrible, crucial mistake. She'd turned off the security and then had left the front door unattended while she took care to put her gun away. It had only been for a minute, but apparently that's all it had taken for Gary to slip inside.

"Gary, what are you doing here?" she asked, trying to buy some time, trying to figure out what to do. Her first thought was for Emily, who was pressed tightly against her side as if sensing danger.

But Brittany knew why he was here and she also knew that her gun was too far away to use for protection. "Gary, let Emily go," she said urgently. "She doesn't know what's happening. Just let her walk out the front door."

"Not a chance," he replied as he advanced closer. "You know what time it is, Brittany."

Emily clung tighter to her side, making it impossible for her to attempt to defend them. "Gary, stop now and nothing will happen to you," Brittany said in an attempt to reason with the young man. "Just leave now and everything will be fine."

He grinned, that open, friendly smile that obviously hid the darkness in his soul. "Nothing is going to happen to me, Brittany."

He was close…too close. She knew the Taser could be effective up to fifteen feet away from its target and he was much closer to her and Emily than that.

"What time is it, Brittany?" Gary asked as he raised the gun and pointed it at her.

"No," she whispered.

"It's party time."

He fired the Taser and instant pain crashed through Brittany. It not only roared through every nerve in her body, but fried in her brain as she felt herself crash to the floor in front of the sofa.

As she felt herself convulsing the only sound she heard was the sound of Emily screaming and then Gary was next to her, a syringe in his hand. She could do nothing as he injected her with something. Emily screamed again and then there was nothing but silence.

Chapter 11

"I feel so foolish," Rose said as she and Alex left the hospital. It was almost eleven and the moon played peekaboo amid a bank of clouds.

"Don't be silly. Angina isn't anything to take lightly," he replied as he led her to his car in the parking lot of the small hospital.

"I sure thought it was a heart attack. I've never felt anything quite so painful."

Alex took her by the arm, grateful that it had been nothing more serious. "I'm just glad you're okay now."

"I hate that you've been sitting in the waiting room so long. It felt like they ran every test imaginable while you just had to sit in that dreadful waiting room. You know I don't like to be a bother."

Alex opened the passenger door of his car for her. "You know you could never be a bother."

He closed the door after she was safely tucked inside and then walked around to the driver door. He assumed by this time Emily was probably asleep.

He felt bad about taking advantage of Brittany, especially given the fact that she'd basically told him to kiss off, but when he'd received the frantic phone call from Rose he hadn't known where else to turn.

"Hopefully Emily hasn't run Brittany completely ragged," Rose said as he started up the car.

"I'm sure Brittany handled things just fine."

As he pulled out of the parking lot he felt Rose's gaze lingering on him. "You like her," she said.

"I'm in love with her," he replied, and then flashed Rose a rueful smile. "It's a bit awkward confessing that to you."

"Shouldn't be," she said in her usual no-nonsense voice. "I know you loved my Linda, but she's gone and you have a life to live and plenty of love to give. How does she feel about you?"

He sighed, a hollow wind blowing through him. "I thought things were moving along nicely. I thought she might even be falling for me, but she told me from the very beginning she wasn't interested in marriage or a ready-made family, and today she made it more than clear that there was no future there."

"I'm sorry, Alex. I want you to have the kind of love and happiness that you deserve, the kind that Linda wasn't capable of giving to you."

He shot her a look of surprise and she smiled. "Alex, I loved my daughter with all my heart and soul, but that doesn't mean I didn't see her weaknesses, her flaws. She was beautiful and achingly fragile. She was like that as a little girl and she never really grew up to be a woman. I want you to find a woman, Alex, a passionate woman who can embrace all of life as you and Emily do."

He'd thought he'd found that woman in Brittany and even now he wasn't sure how he was going to live his life to the fullest without her in it.

When he reached Rose's house he insisted he walk her inside and get her comfortable. As she went into her bedroom to change into her nightclothes and a robe he stood at the front door and stared out into the night.

It had been a tough day. He'd tried to keep a happy face on for Emily after he'd gotten home from Brittany's, but even the little girl had sensed his unhappiness.

How could something that had felt so right turn out to be so wrong? Why was she so certain she couldn't be a mother? She was terrific with Emily and he knew his daughter was already more than half in love with her.

Had she thrown them aside because of the danger that surrounded her? Maybe that's what this afternoon had been, her attempt to protect them.

The thought put a little bit of hope in his heart. Or maybe he was fooling himself and she just plain didn't love him. The tiny blossom of hope withered and died away.

He couldn't do anything about it now. He'd pretty much laid his heart on the line and she'd kicked it to the curb and at this point whatever her reason, the end result was the same.

Rose came out of her bedroom clad in her long, flowered robe. "Thank you, Alex. I don't know what I would have done without you tonight."

He kissed her on the forehead. "I don't know what Emily and I would do without you."

"Now go on, get out of here. I'll be fine here. Get that child of yours and get some sleep and I'll talk to you in the morning."

Within minutes he was back in his car and headed to Brittany's place. He gripped the steering wheel tightly, preparing himself for seeing her again.

He'd lived through the death of a wife. He'd survived dealing with a grieving daughter. He'd dealt with girly tears and learning to French braid and yet the thought of seeing Brittany again suddenly terrified him.

He pulled up in her driveway and saw the lights shining from the front window. Emily was probably still awake, treating the night like a special slumber party.

He got out of the car and walked to the front door and then knocked, surprised when he didn't hear any sound of movement from inside.

"Brittany, Emily, it's me," he said as he rapped harder on the door. The resulting silence set off the first alarm in his head. Brittany wouldn't have gone anywhere with Emily at this time of night. They should be in there and he couldn't imagine that they would both be sleeping so soundly they wouldn't hear him at the front door.

He rang the doorbell several times and then pounded on the door with his fist, the alarm growing louder in his head.

When there was still no answer he grabbed the front doorknob and to his surprise it twisted and opened. No sound to indicate a breach of the security.

Heart pounding, he stepped inside. "Brittany! Emily?" he cried out even though he knew they weren't there. The house held the silence of a person holding their breath…a silence that absolutely terrified him.

He raced through the house, just to make sure that he was right, that they weren't there. Brittany's car was in the garage and her purse was slung over the back of a kitchen chair. It was when he saw the purse that he went to the phone and called the sheriff's office.

Thankfully it was Tom who answered the phone. "Tom, you've got to get to Brittany's house right away. Something is wrong. I just got here and the door was unlocked, the security wasn't on and she's not here. Her car is here, her purse is here, but she's not." His voice cracked as emotion swelled up inside him. "She was babysitting my daughter. They're gone, Tom. They're both gone."

The minutes were agonizing as he waited for Tom to arrive. He stood in the center of the living room where he imagined he could smell the scent of Brittany's perfume, the sweet strawberry scent of his daughter's hair.

It was easy to see how the two had spent part of their time together during the evening. Bottles of fingernail polish littered the top of the coffee table. What he couldn't make sense of were the small multi-colored tabs that littered the floor, looking like pink, yellow and white confetti from an abandoned party.

He touched nothing, except his heart, slamming his hand against it in an effort to control the frantic beat. His knees felt weak and he had to consciously tighten his knees to keep him upright.

What had happened here? Who could have gotten in with the security? Where was his daughter? Where was Brittany?

Tom didn't arrive alone. He had all three brothers with him and they entered the house as if entering a war zone. With grim faces and dark eyes, they strode into the living room looking as if they wanted to find somebody to kill.

It took precious moments for Alex to explain the events of the night: Rose's heart attack scare, him bringing Emily here and then his race to the hospital.

"Taser markers," Benjamin said as he bent down and picked up one of the yellow pieces of confetti.

Alex's heart seemed to stop in his chest. "What are you talking about?"

"When a Taser is fired it deploys little identification markers," Caleb said.

"So, you can tell by those who the Taser belongs to?" Alex asked hopefully.

"If it was bought legally, which I seriously doubt," Benjamin replied.

"We have to do something," Alex exclaimed. He felt as if he were about to jump out of his skin. They needed to find Brittany. And God…dear God, he needed them to find his daughter.

"We start by processing the scene," Tom said. "Did you touch anything?"

"Nothing—except for the phone to call you," Alex replied.

"Then stand out of the way and let us do our jobs."

Alex stood in the foyer as they all began to collect evidence, talking in hushed tones that did nothing to ease Alex's fear.

He felt as if he were dying a slow death, as if everything and everyone were moving in slow motion. He wanted to scream at them to hurry up, to do whatever it took to find his daughter and Brittany.

Caleb left and Alex knew he was probably going to canvass the neighborhood, to see if anyone had seen anything, had heard anything that might let them know who to look for.

But where would they even begin to look? He knew there wasn't even a suspect on their radar. They had no idea who might be responsible for whatever had happened here tonight.

A darkness swept through Alex as he realized they might already be too late. He might have already lost not just the woman he loved, but the daughter who was his heart, his very soul.

* * *

The Real Professional looked at the two unconscious bodies in his shed. He'd done it! It had been pure, sweet fate that had allowed him to sneak into Brittany's house, to see her reset the alarm after the little girl had come inside and to hide in her coat closet until the time he'd stepped out and confronted them.

The Taser had done the initial work and then the drug he'd used had done the rest, rendering them both unconscious while he got them loaded into his vehicle.

The setup in the shed wasn't ideal. He didn't have the finances that Larry Norwood had possessed. He hadn't been able to build separate cells. Instead the two were shackled to the wall with iron ankle rings. He'd provided a portable toilet that could be reached by the length of their chain. He'd give them food and water.

He could keep them here as long or as short of a time as he desired. Emily had been a surprise...a gift that would certainly ensure that his name would be written in the annals of famous criminals.

The Professional hadn't taken a child. But The Real Professional had and that made him badder and better. Excitement roared through his veins. If he stuck to the plan, then he'd need to take several more women before he had his own "party." But he wasn't sure he could wait that long. He wasn't sure he wanted to wait that long.

Chapter 12

Consciousness came slowly. Brittany's first thought was that she'd been hit by a car or had been in some sort of terrible accident. Every muscle in her body ached and her head banged with a nauseating intensity.

She couldn't open her eyes...not yet. She was afraid that a shaft of sunlight, an overhead lamp might make her skull split in two.

She must have fallen back asleep, for when she became conscious once again her head felt a little better. The banging was down to a manageable ache. Then the memories slammed into her brain, retrieving her headache with a vengeance.

Gary. The Taser.

Emily!

Her eyes flew open and in an instant she took in her

surroundings. An old shed. No cages, but her ankle was shackled to the wall with a thick chain.

Emily was curled up on the floor next to her, unusually pale and not moving. *Don't be dead,* Brittany thought anxiously. *Oh, please, don't be dead.* She touched Emily's arm, encouraged by the warmth of her skin.

"Emily?" she whispered.

The little girl stirred but didn't wake up. Brittany decided to let her stay sleeping. There was no question that they'd been drugged. Brittany could still feel the aftereffects—a touch of nausea and the feeling of cotton wrapped around her brain.

But she needed to peel back the cotton and take stock of their surroundings. She needed to find a way out, to get Emily to safety.

But before she could think, before she could plan, a wave of despair rushed over her. How could this be happening again? What were the odds of being held captive by a madman twice in a lifetime?

Tears burned at her eyes but she willed them away. She didn't have time to cry. She had to figure out a way to get Emily out of here. If Brittany had to die in this shed, then so be it, but Emily was just a child and somehow, someway she had to be saved.

Sucking up the tears that still threatened to fall, Brittany took a look around. The wooden shed where they were being held was old and relatively small and had probably once been used for storage.

She saw the portable toilet nearby and a new chill danced over her skin. That indicated a lengthy stay. She also saw that there were three more shackles bolted into the walls, all empty and awaiting new victims.

So, Gary had intended to emulate his hero as closely as possible by kidnapping five women, but he obviously hadn't had the financial means to make this place as spiffy as Larry had made his holding area.

She tested the shackle around her ankle, unsurprised that it was fastened tight and impossible to slip. She was also not surprised to see that it was securely bolted to the wall, bolted tightly enough that it would take more than her bare hands and strength to get it loose.

With a sigh she leaned back against the wall. Gary. Her mind still couldn't wrap around the fact that it had been red-haired, freckled Gary behind all this.

What worried her more than anything was that Gary would probably be the last person her brothers would look at as a potential suspect. Although he had been hanging around her house to work, he was so young and appeared to be friendly and eager to please. But that was obviously a facade that hid a malevolent darkness well.

She didn't have her watch on and so had no idea what time it might be. A small bare lightbulb dangled from the ceiling burned in one corner of the shed, illuminating the interior, but it had to be after midnight.

She had no idea where they were, where this shed was located. She didn't know how long she'd been unconscious, didn't know if they were still anywhere near Black Rock. She didn't know enough about Gary's background. She didn't even know where he lived.

It was possible nobody even knew they were missing yet. Alex might still be at the hospital with Rose, not knowing that his daughter was in danger.

She glanced back at Emily, who still seemed to be sleeping soundly. Fine, let her sleep through the night. Let her sleep as long as possible before she had to wake up and face this nightmare that had caught them unaware.

She tensed as she heard the sound of footsteps approaching. Gary stepped through the door, that goofy, friendly smile on his face and a plastic grocery sack looped over one arm. "Ah, I see you're awake."

"What are you doing, Gary? Let us go and I'll see that you get some help."

His smile widened. "The way I see it I'm not the one who needs help, but you look like you could use a little. Unfortunately, if I were you I wouldn't hold my breath waiting for it to come."

"Let Emily go. If you think you're re-creating Larry's crimes, he never hurt a child. He never took a child."

Gary's blue eyes lit with an electric fire. "I know. Killing her just makes me better than him. People in this town will talk about me long after I'm gone."

"What good will it do you? You'll be dead, just like Larry."

The smile fell from his lips. "Oh, no, nobody is going to catch me. I'm smarter than Larry, better than him. I'll be like the Zodiac killer," he said, referencing a serial killer who had become famous in the late 1960s and early 1970s and who had never been identified or caught. "Honestly, Brittany, who is going to suspect me?" He flashed her that bright smile once again.

He tossed the grocery bag in her direction and it landed just to the left of her. She was almost afraid to look inside. "That should hold you until I get back here," he said. "You know, I'm not completely like him. I don't have to have an audience to enjoy my work. I could kill you right now and start my own legend."

It took every ounce of Brittany's control not to explode, not to scream and rant at him, but she didn't want to awaken Emily, who continued to sleep next to her.

Gary grinned. "Guess I'll let you live for the night. We'll just have to wait to see what tomorrow brings." With those frightening words he stepped away from the door and disappeared into the darkness of the night.

For several long minutes Brittany sat staring at the darkness just outside the doorway, every muscle in her body taut, an ache in the back of her head threatening to make her sick.

They were obviously far enough out of town that he wasn't worried about them screaming for help, otherwise they would be gagged. The small town of Black Rock was surrounded by farmland with hundreds of sheds abandoned and left to rot.

She and Emily could be in any one of those places, far enough away that their screams couldn't be heard, yet close enough to safety to run to it if they could just get free of the chains that held them.

Remembering the bag that Gary had thrown at her,

she picked it up and looked inside. A couple of bottles of water, two snack-size bags of chips and what appeared to be two cheese sandwiches in bags.

At that moment Emily moaned and her eyelids fluttered and then opened. A little frown danced across her forehead as she looked around and then a sharp cry of alarm escaped her.

"Emily, it's okay, honey. I'm here." Brittany wrapped the little girl in her arms and held her tight. "I'm right here with you."

Emily clung to her and Brittany didn't know if it was the little girl's heartbeat that pounded so frantically or her own. "I don't have Lady Bear," Emily said, her voice quivering with the portent of tears.

"No, you don't. But you have me." Brittany tightened her embrace around Emily.

Emily leaned into her and released a tremulous sigh. "We're in big trouble, aren't we?"

Brittany hesitated. She didn't want to frighten Emily any more than she already was, but she also didn't want to blatantly lie to her. "Yes, we're in trouble, but I'm hoping your daddy or one of my brothers will find us very soon and get us out of trouble."

Emily sat up and looked at her. "Do you think they can find us?"

"I think it's possible." Brittany tried to inject as much hope as she could in her voice.

Emily's gaze went out the door. "It's nighttime."

"Yes, honey, it is."

"Maybe daddy will be here first thing in the morning."

"That's right. So it would be best if we both tried to get some sleep," Brittany replied, although sleep was the very last thing on her mind.

"Okay." Once again Emily leaned against Brittany and closed her eyes. She was quiet and still only a moment and then sat back up with a sigh. "I can't sleep. I'm scared." She looked at Brittany with her beautiful green eyes. "Maybe if we talk for a little longer I can get sleepy."

"Okay, what do you want to talk about?"

For the next half an hour they talked about favorite colors and what Emily wanted to be when she grew up. She wasn't sure if she wanted to be a ballerina or one of the people who arrested people who were mean to dogs and cats.

"I want a dog," she said, her voice getting drowsy. "Maybe you could help me talk Daddy into getting one. Lady Bear would like a dog."

Brittany smoothed a strand of her hair away from Emily's face. "We'll have to talk to your daddy about that."

She should be trying to figure out a way to get them out of here. She should be frantically yanking on the bolts that held the chains to the wall, screaming her fool head off in case somebody might hear and come to their rescue. But at the moment she felt as if the most important thing she could do in the world was keep Emily's terror at bay.

"Daddy is going to be so mad at Gary." Emily leaned heavier against Brittany's side.

"Yes, he is." Brittany moved her hand from stroking Emily's hair to caressing her back. Emily sighed.

"How come you aren't a mommy?"

"I'm not sure I'd know how to be a mommy," Brittany replied.

"Oh, I'm sure you'd make a wonderful mommy," Emily replied, her voice slightly slurry with the edges of sleep creeping in. "And what you don't know about it, I could teach you."

Brittany couldn't speak, not with her heart so big, so tight in her chest, and within another minute she knew that Emily was once again asleep.

Tears once again burned at her eyes as she thought of Alex, who'd already lost his wife. She didn't want him to lose his child, too.

Somehow she had to figure out a way to get Emily out of here alive. No matter what it took, she had to save Emily.

The night was endless. When the sun began its rise Alex stood at Brittany's living-room window and watched it with eyes that burned from lack of sleep, from the beginning edges of a grief the likes of which he'd never known.

Tom was in the kitchen, coordinating the search for Brittany and Emily from there. Caleb and Benjamin were out walking the streets, trying to glean any information that might help them find out who was responsible for the kidnappings. Tom had assigned another deputy to sit at Alex's house just in case the kidnapper might try to make contact there.

Alex wanted to be home. He wanted to sit in Emily's room and smell the scent of her that lingered in the air, needed to be in his familiar surroundings while his entire world fell apart.

Here the scent of Brittany that lingered in the air ripped at his heart, but Tom wanted him here, along with Jacob. Larry Norwood had taken great pleasure in calling Jacob Grayson and taunting him about the crimes he was going to commit. They were all hoping that if this was a copycat kind of situation, then the perp would try to make contact with Jacob once again.

Jacob sat on the sofa, his cell phone in his lap and dark anger in his eyes. Alex could definitely relate to the anger. If he shoved aside his fear, he knew there was a rage building inside him, a rage that scared him just a little bit with its ferocity.

He turned away from the window to face Jacob. "I love her, you know."

Jacob nodded his head slightly. "She sounds like a cute kid."

Alex frowned. "Of course I love my daughter, but I'm talking about your sister."

"She's a cute kid, too."

"She's not a kid." Some of the frustration Alex felt crept into his voice. "She's a loving, caring woman and it's high time all of you treat her like one."

Jacob raised a dark eyebrow. "Hey, I'm on your side, remember?"

Alex felt his face warm. "Sorry," he said. "I just feel like I'm about to jump out of my skin." He turned back to the window. "Where could they be? Who in the hell is responsible for this?"

"We'll figure it out," Jacob replied, but there was no real conviction in his deep voice.

It was almost ten when Caleb came in. Alex followed him into the kitchen where Tom sat at the table, a stack of notes in front of him, notes Alex knew were from the original crimes.

"Luke Mathis has a solid alibi for last night. Even though he was off work at Harley's he spent the entire night there drinking so heavily that when the bar closed Harley let him sleep on a cot in the break room," Caleb said. "He was still there, still half-drunk when I talked to him a little while ago."

A wave of hopelessness blew through Alex. He'd hoped…he'd really hoped that Luke was behind all this and that Emily had just been in the wrong place at the wrong time when an ex-lover had decided to confront Brittany.

Tom released a heavy sigh. "So, that takes care of our one and only suspect."

"What about Buck?" Alex asked suddenly.

"What about him?" Tom asked.

"He was working here with me. He asked some inappropriate questions to Brittany about her time with Larry Norwood, seemed way too excited to talk about what she'd been through."

A deep frown cut across Tom's forehead. "Buck might be a lot of things, but I can't quite see him being responsible for this. Still…" He picked up his cell phone. "Let's get him in here and have a discussion with him."

"Wait," Alex said. "Let me call him. I'll tell him

I need an hour or so of work from him. He won't be suspicious if I call and he's always up for a little extra pay."

Buck answered on the second ring. "Hey, boss, what's up?"

"I've got a little more cleanup here at Brittany's and wondered if you could come and help. I don't need anyone but you and it will only take a few minutes." Alex was pleased that his voice didn't betray any of the turmoil inside him.

"When do you need me?"

"As soon as you can get here," Alex replied.

"I'll be there in about fifteen minutes."

The call ended and Alex looked at Tom. "He's on his way. But what if he doesn't have them? What if he isn't a part of this?"

"Then we keep looking and we hope we get lucky," Tom replied.

"If he's playing the game like the original, then he won't hurt them until he has more women," Caleb said. "At least that works in our favor."

"But he's already deviated from the original. Larry Norwood never took a child," Alex said, the words falling like painful glass shards from his mouth.

"And maybe he'll let Emily go," Tom said in an obvious effort to soothe Alex. But there was no soothing. There was nothing that could ease Alex's terror, his grief until both his daughter and Brittany were out of harm's way.

By the time Buck arrived Alex was ready to tear off

somebody's head. The rage was taking hold, so much easier to embrace than the killing grief and fear.

Buck knocked on the back door and Alex opened the door, grabbed him by the arm and pulled him into the kitchen. "Where's my daughter?"

"What?" Buck look around the room, his gaze lingering on Tom, then Caleb and finally back to Alex. "Wha—what's going on here?"

"Somebody broke in here last night and kidnapped Brittany and Emily," Tom said. He gestured to a chair at the table. "Sit down, Buck. We need to have a little chat."

"You think I had something to do with this?" Buck cursed soundly. "Why is it that anytime anything goes wrong in this stupid town you come to me? I don't know anything about it. Why would I want to do something like that?"

"Maybe because Larry Norwood was your hero. Maybe you want to be just like him." Alex's need to punch somebody was overwhelming, but instead he fisted his hands at his sides.

"What, are you crazy?" Buck looked at him in astonishment. "Norwood was a sick twist. Why would I want to be anything like him?"

"You seemed very interested in Brittany's experience with him," Alex countered.

"Sure, I've never known anyone who's been held by a serial killer. I was curious." Buck frowned. "But I'm not the only one. Gary talks about The Professional all the time."

"Gary?" Tom looked at Alex.

"Gary Cox. He's the other kid I used to help build Brittany's deck," Alex replied.

"But Gary wouldn't do something like this," Buck said with a half laugh. "He's just a goofy kid."

Gary was just a goofy kid and from what Alex had heard Larry Norwood was a nice man who cared for animals. You never knew what kind of facade hid the heart of a killer.

"Where does Gary live?" Tom asked.

"In the same apartment complex where I live. But he's almost never home." Buck's eyes narrowed. "He spends a lot of time working on an old abandoned shed he says he's turning into some kind of an awesome man cave."

Alex's heart jumped as Caleb and Tom exchanged glances. "Where is this shed?" Tom asked as he got out of his chair.

"I've never been there, but I know it's someplace on the Burwell property," Buck replied.

"The Burwell property?" Alex looked at Tom.

"Raymond Burwell died a little over a year ago without a will, leaving his farm tied up in probate court with relatives all fighting over it. It's a big spread, overgrown and with several outbuildings," Tom said.

"Then let's go," Alex exclaimed with a sick urgency pressing tight against his chest. He felt sick to his stomach, so afraid that this all might be a wild-goose chase, so afraid that they were already too late.

Chapter 13

Emily had slept through the rest of the night but Brittany had found sleep impossible. As she'd held Emily close her thoughts had gone in every direction possible.

She'd relived those days...weeks when she'd been held captive by Larry Norwood and reminded herself that she'd survived once before and she could do it again.

If the very worst happened and she didn't get out of this shed alive at least she'd had those moments in Alex's arms, those moments when she'd felt more alive, more loved, than she ever had in her life.

She could have loved Alex if she'd allowed herself to. She could have easily envisioned a future with him. He was everything she'd ever wanted in a man.

She smiled as she thought about Emily telling her she could teach her whatever she needed to learn about being a mother. Her smile fell. Emily was obviously so hungry for a stepmother, she had no standards whatsoever.

Funny, the last time she'd been held against her will she'd thought about building a deck and spending time with friends and family. This time she thought about love and being in Alex's arms.

Brittany guessed that it was about nine in the morning when Emily woke up. She sat up and rubbed her eyes. "I thought it was all a bad dream, but it's real, isn't it? Do you think Daddy will come soon?"

"I hope so. Are you hungry?" Brittany opened the bag and pulled out a bottle of water and a bag of the chips. She was afraid of the sandwiches, which weren't prepackaged.

"I'm not really hungry. I just want my daddy and my Lady Bear," Emily said in a tiny whisper.

"I know, honey." Brittany pulled her back into her arms and for several long minutes neither of them spoke.

"You know what?" Emily finally asked.

"What?"

"I think if I point my toes like a ballerina I can slip my foot out of this thing around my ankle."

Brittany's heart began a rapid tattoo. "Really? You want to try it and see?"

Emily bent down and unlaced the tennis shoe she wore. The sight of her pink polka-dot socks nearly made Brittany lose it. No little girl in pink polka-dot socks should be in this place, at the mercy of a young man who was obviously unbalanced.

Once the shoe was off Emily pointed her toe just like a ballerina and she could easily pull it out of the shackle that was intended for an adult's foot.

Brittany's heart nearly exploded. Emily was free! She could run and get help. But wait… Brittany's head whirled with suppositions. What if Gary was right outside the building? What if he lived close enough that he would see if Emily ran outside? The last thing Brittany wanted was for Emily to run into more harm.

A plan began to formulate in her head, a dangerous plan that might get them both killed or could possibly be their salvation. As she heard footsteps approaching the shed she quickly whispered her plan, not once, but twice, to Emily. She prayed the little girl understood and obeyed. It might be their only hope.

With Emily's stockinged foot covered by the plastic bag that had held their food and her tennis shoe behind Brittany's back, Brittany prepared to meet the devil in his lair.

Gary appeared in the doorway, his bright smile like nails on a chalkboard screeching up Brittany's spine. "Well, looks like you both made it through the night."

"You're a bad man," Emily said, surprising Brittany with her show of bravado. "You're a bad man and you're going to get punished."

Gary laughed. "You got a little smart mouth on you, girl. What are you going to do? Put me in time-out?"

"And you've got delusions of grandeur, Gary," Brittany said, wanting to take his attention off Emily.

"You're just a freckle-faced punk pretending to be a bad guy."

Gary's nostrils pinched together, letting her know her remark had gotten under his skin. "You know what's interesting about serial killers? Nobody ever remembers the names of the victims, but they always remember the name of the killer."

"Oh, yeah, and have you picked your killer name yet?" She kept a taunting tone in her voice. She had to make him mad. She had to make him mad enough to get closer to her. "Maybe Howdy Doody or Tom Sawyer?"

"You've got a smart mouth on you, too," Gary said, no longer smiling. "I'm The Real Professional." He said the words as if he were proclaiming himself the King of Siam.

Brittany forced herself to laugh, as if finding him immensely amusing. "Gary, Gary, nobody is going to remember your name. A year from now nobody here or anywhere else on the planet will give you a minute's thought, except maybe your parents, who will wonder for the rest of their lives where they went wrong."

"My parents don't give a crap about me," he scoffed.

"Ah, poor baby, so you're planning on using the 'I've been neglected and abused by my parents and that turned me into a monster' defense. Larry Norwood was The Professional—you're not even a pale imitation."

Her heart jumped as he took a step toward her. She felt Emily tense next to her and prayed the child remembered every single detail of their plan, prayed that Emily would do exactly what Brittany had told her to do.

"Shut up," he said as he narrowed his eyes and took another step closer to her.

Just one more step or two and he'd be close enough. Her heart screamed in her chest. She forced a laugh again. "At least Larry had a real place to keep us, with cells and cots to sleep on. He was a genius. He pulled off his plot in Kansas City and almost got away with it here. You'll never be like him, Gary. You'll always be just a pathetic pretender. Hey, there's a name for you, The Pathetic Pretender."

He lunged at her, rage twisting his features into something unrecognizable. Brittany was ready for him. She wrapped her arms tight around him, gripping him at the knees with all the strength she possessed.

"Run!" she screamed at Emily at the same time Gary's fist crashed down on Brittany's head.

Emily scrambled to her feet and ran. As she disappeared out the door Brittany tightened her arms around Gary's knees, keeping him from chasing after the child.

Run, baby, run, she thought as Gary delivered a blow that struck her upside the face. The pain crashed through her. She tasted blood and almost immediately felt her lip swell, but she didn't loosen her grip on him. She knew the longer she could hang on the more of a chance Emily had to get away.

Run fast, she thought. *Get as far away from here*

as possible. Despite her pain her heart swelled with the hope that Emily had truly escaped.

Gary railed like a madman, screaming and cursing as he hit her again and again. He smashed his fists into her ribs, slammed her in the gut over and over again.

She sobbed with the pain, afraid that he would beat her to death if she didn't let go of him, but knowing if she let go he'd run after Emily.

Finally he delivered a blow to her head that made stars dance in front of her eyes and a sickening nausea well up inside her. In horror she felt her arms slipping from him and her last conscious thought was that she hoped she'd given Emily enough time to get away.

As the men prepared to leave Brittany's house, Alex realized they didn't intend for him to go with them. Tom had been on his phone, arranging for several other deputies to meet them at the Burwell property.

As Tom walked out the front door and headed for his car, Alex caught up to him. "I'm coming with you."

"You're a civilian. It's best if you stay here and wait," Tom replied.

"Not going to happen." Alex met the man stare for stare. "It's my daughter, Tom. And it's the woman I love. I can either ride with you or I can follow you in my car, but there's no way in hell I'm staying here."

Without waiting for Tom's reply Alex slid into the passenger seat of his car. "You're a stubborn cuss, aren't you?" Tom said as he got behind the wheel and started the car. "I suppose you'll have to be if you plan on sticking around Brittany for any length of time."

They both fell silent as Tom pulled out of the driveway and tore down the street with Brittany's brothers following in their own vehicles.

A hard knot sat where Alex's heart should be. What if they were headed in the wrong direction? What if they were too late?

He couldn't think that. He couldn't imagine his life without his Emily. She was the best part of him, the very core of the heart that beat in his chest.

And Brittany, how his heart ached with thoughts of her. It didn't matter if she couldn't see herself in his life, he just needed to know that she was someplace on earth living in the kind of happiness she deserved.

The drive to the Burwell place seemed to take forever and when they arrived at the small farmhouse all the law-enforcement officials gathered around Tom.

"If Gary is the person we're looking for then we have to assume that he's armed and dangerous," Tom said. "I want us to search in teams of two." As he assigned the areas he gestured toward Alex. "You stay with me."

Alex nodded, eager to get started, hoping and praying that they were at the right place at the right time. Any other thought was simply too painful to entertain.

"I want us to go in quietly," Tom continued. "Put your phones on vibrate and keep your eyes and ears open." With those final words the men all parted ways.

Alex wanted to run through the overgrown grass toward the half a dozen outbuilding in the distance.

He wanted to rip open doors, tear at old lumber, do whatever it took to find Gary Cox's man cave.

Was Gary simply building a place to party? A place where he could bring his friends to drink and play music and not have to worry about the complaints of neighbors?

As he and Tom grew closer to one of the buildings, Alex recognized Gary's car parked nearby. The knot in his chest twisted tighter.

Okay, so the kid was here, but that didn't mean Emily and Brittany were here, as well. Tom had his gun drawn, his eyes cold and dark as they drew closer to the building.

They paused just outside the door and that's when Alex heard it—the sound of a man cursing softly, the moan of somebody hurt and the sound of fist meeting flesh.

All cautions that Tom had given his men, any orders Alex was meant to follow, flew out of his head. With the adrenaline of an enraged bull, Alex flew inside the building.

In an instant he summed up the nightmarish scene. Gary stood over Brittany with his fist raised to deliver another blow. Her face was bloodied and she looked unconscious and there was no sign of Emily.

He didn't make a sound as he attacked. He grabbed Gary by the shoulder, whirled him around and then delivered a punch to the center of his face. As Gary stumbled back and fell to the ground Alex wasn't finished yet. He leaped on top of Gary's prone body and began to pummel, all his fear, his anger centered in his fists.

"What did you do to Brittany? And where's Emily?" he screamed as he pounded. "Where's my daughter?"

"If you kill him he won't be able to tell you," Tom exclaimed as he pulled Alex up and off Gary.

Alex immediately rushed to Brittany. Her mouth was bloody, one of her eyes blackened and swollen shut. She seemed to be hanging on to consciousness by a mere thread, but at least she was alive.

Alex whirled back to face Gary, who Tom had gotten to his feet and handcuffed. "Where's Emily?" he asked, vaguely aware of the shed filling with Brittany's brothers and some of the other deputies.

"I killed the little brat," Gary said as Tom dug through his pockets for the key to the shackle that bound Brittany to the wall. "I killed her and buried her body in the field outside."

"No, he's lying." The words left Brittany on a soft pain-laced whisper. "She got away. I held him so she could run as fast and as far away as possible. Go, Alex, she's somewhere out there and she needs her daddy."

At that moment the scream of a siren sounded from the distance and Alex realized one of the brothers had called for an ambulance. Brittany would be cared for, but he had to find his daughter. "Thank you," he said, knowing the words would never be enough to convey his gratitude for the woman he knew had saved his daughter's life.

He tore out of the shed, unsure in which direction to run. Had Gary beaten Emily, too? Was she lying in the tall grass somewhere slowly dying?

"Emily!" He screamed her name as tears began to blur his vision. The overgrown brush and weeds were so tall and she was so little. "Emily, where are you?" The words tore from his throat, from a place of such pain he nearly fell to his knees.

As the ambulance pulled up, several of the other men left the shed and began to search, as well, calling out Emily's name. It was such a big field and there was no way to know what direction she might have run, how far she might have been able to go in whatever time she'd had.

Agonizing minutes passed with Alex continuing to yell her name until he was half-hoarse. He couldn't think about Brittany's injuries. The thought of her bloodied features made him want to weep, but knowing she was being attended to, he had to stay focused on Emily.

And then she was there…rising out of the tall grass in front of him. Her green eyes wide and filled with tears. "Daddy?"

Alex fell to his knees and opened his arms and she ran to him. He wrapped his arms around her and squeezed her tight, sobbing into her hair as relief coursed through him.

"I knew you'd come, Daddy. I just knew it," she whispered fiercely against his ear, her arms wrapped in a near death grip around his neck as she began to cry.

"It's okay, baby." His heart swelled tight in his chest. "You're safe now and Daddy is never going to let anything like this happen to you again." He scooped her up in his arms and rose to his feet.

Benjamin approached them, his relief evident on his handsome features. "I recommend you take her to the hospital, get her checked out by a doctor and then Tom will want to talk to her."

Alex's first impulse was to take her home and never let her go again, but he knew Benjamin was right. She needed to be checked by a doctor and then she'd have to tell her story to Tom.

"It won't take long," Alex said to his daughter. "We'll get some things taken care of and then we'll take you home where Lady Bear is waiting for you."

"I don't want Lady Bear. I just want Brittany," she replied.

So do I, Alex thought. At that moment the ambulance pulled away, sirens screaming as it raced toward the main road. He had no idea what kind of internal injuries she might have suffered. She'd looked half-dead from the beating she'd taken.

"Let's get out of here," Alex said.

Gary was taken away by Caleb as Tom offered to take Alex and Emily to the hospital. As they made the drive Tom asked Emily questions and it didn't take long for a picture of what had gone down to appear.

It also didn't take long to realize that Brittany had sacrificed herself for Emily's escape. "She held on to him so he couldn't run after me and he hit her hard, but she screamed at me to run," Emily said as she rubbed tears from her cheeks.

If Alex had believed himself in love with Brittany before, this information only intensified the depth of his love for her. He couldn't wait to find out how she was, but it was a long process when they arrived at the hospital.

Emily got a clean bill of health and then they sat in the waiting room to hear word about Brittany. Emily sat on his lap, curled into his chest and sharing bits and pieces of the long night with him.

"I think I lost my shoe," she said and pointed at her stockinged foot.

"We'll get you a new pair of shoes," Alex replied. "We'll get you a dozen pairs of new shoes."

"I just need one pair. Daddy, I would have really been scared, but Brittany made me feel not so scared. When can I see her?"

"I'm hoping soon," he replied. He needed to see her, to thank her for what she'd done for Emily…for him.

It was another hour before Jacob finally came into the waiting room. Emily was almost asleep, but she perked right up at the sight of the lawman and the news that she could go see Brittany.

"She's going to be fine, although she's banged up pretty good," he said. He looked at Emily. "She has a black eye and her mouth is kind of puffy, so she doesn't look too good." Alex appreciated him warning Emily. "They're going to keep her overnight for observation, but you can go see her if you want. Room 112."

Emily scrambled off Alex's lap, as if not wanting to wait another minute. Alex had to hurry to keep up with her as she raced toward Brittany's room.

She turned into the room and then stopped and gasped with her hands over her mouth. Alex nearly bumped into her and his heart cried as he saw Brittany. One side of her face was black-and-blue, that eye swollen shut. Her mouth was swollen, with a cut on the corner but she offered them both a wobbly smile.

She looks like this because she saved my daughter, Alex thought. Her sacrifice weakened his knees, ached in his chest. He was positively humbled by the half-broken woman in the hospital bed.

"Oh, Brittany," Emily exclaimed as she lowered her hands and raced to the side of the bed. "You look awful."

"It doesn't hurt as bad as it looks," Brittany replied drowsily. "They gave me a shot that pretty much made the pain go away."

"I don't know how to thank you," Alex began, his voice thick with emotion.

Brittany held up a hand to stop whatever he was going to say. "Please, just let it go."

"At least your fingernails still look pretty," Emily said as she moved to the side of Brittany's bed. Alex noticed that Brittany's nails were each a different color, obviously his daughter's handiwork.

"Can I give you a hug?" Emily asked.

"Honey, I don't think that's a good idea," Alex protested.

"I think it's a wonderful idea," Brittany replied, her

voice slurring slightly. To Alex's surprise she patted the bed next to her.

Emily crawled up on the bed and curled into Brittany's side. Brittany placed an arm around her as Emily ever so gently kissed her on the cheek. "I love you, Brittany," Emily said softly.

"I love you, too," Brittany whispered softly as she closed her eyes. Within minutes both of the women who held Alex's heart were sound asleep.

When Brittany awakened she was alone in the hospital bed. The room was semidark with only the light from the sinking sun coming in through the window. Alex sat in the chair next to her bed and he smiled at her as he realized she was awake.

"Emily?" she asked.

"Is with Rose," he replied.

"Gary?"

"Is in jail."

She sat up, wincing as every ache and pain in her body made themselves known. "And all is right with the world."

"I don't know how to thank you for what you did. You saved Emily's life."

There was such emotion in his eyes, those beautiful blue eyes that she'd thought she'd never see again. "I was just doing my job. And it is going to be my job again. I've decided to go back to being a deputy."

"That's good if that's where your heart is," he replied.

"It is."

"So, you feel competent enough to keep an entire town safe but not enough to help parent a six-year-old little girl who loves you desperately."

He didn't give her a chance to reply, but continued as he got out of his chair and stepped closer to her. "I love you, Brittany, and I believe in my heart that you love me, too. I think we could have something magical between us if you'd just allow it to happen."

"There's a difference between being a deputy and being a mom," she said. There was no place on her body, on her face, that ached more than her heart.

"Yeah, you need a gun to be a deputy, but all you need to have to be a mom is love. You sacrificed yourself for Emily in that shed. You already proved yourself to have a mother's heart."

She stared at him, at the face she'd grown to love. There had been a little part of her that hadn't believed in herself, that had been afraid that she wasn't the woman she wanted to be, the woman he and Emily needed in their lives.

She'd faced not one, but two serial killers and she'd survived. She wasn't crazy and she had grown from the immature girl she used to be into a woman who wanted something meaningful, something lasting in her life. And that something was here right in front of her. All she had to do was reach out and embrace it.

"When we were in that shed, Emily told me that being a mom was easy, but that if I had problems with it she could teach me all I needed to know about it," she said.

Hope lit Alex's eyes and in that hope she saw a

reflection of the woman he saw when he looked at her—a strong woman with a loving heart, a woman ready to take on the responsibilities of a ready-made family.

"Yes," she said.

"Yes, what?" he asked, looking perplexed.

"Yes, I'd like to be a part of your life, of Emily's life. Yes, I want Emily to teach me everything I need to know about being a mom. I love you, Alex, and I'm ready to take care of the town and then come home to a loving family. This thing between us, I'm not ready for it to stop, either."

His eyes blazed with love and desire and he made a sound of frustration. "I desperately want to kiss you, but I'm afraid no matter where I kiss I'll hurt you."

Brittany held up her hand with the multicolored fingernails. He took her hand and brought it to his lips where he kissed each and every finger with a gentleness that promised the kind of happiness Brittany had never dreamed possible.

She was not the child her brothers thought of her as, nor was she simply a victim of the crimes that had been perpetrated against her. She was just a woman in love with a man and his daughter and she was eager to discover the future with them that awaited her.

Epilogue

Chaos reigned on the deck that Alex built. Conversations filled the air along with the heady smoke scent of barbecue. An explosion of colorful flowers lined the deck and tumbled into a flower garden in the yard where Emily was playing with Lilly in the grass.

Nobody complained about the late-July heat, especially not Brittany, who was seeing the final version of the vision that had sustained her when Larry Norwood had held her captive for so long. The only additions to that vision were Alex and Emily.

No matter how long Larry would have held her she never would have been able to imagine the kind of love she'd experienced in the three months since Gary Cox had been arrested.

She and Alex had taken things slow, maintaining their own residences and dating. But her love for him and Emily had blossomed with each day that had passed.

Loving Emily was easy. Loving Alex felt as necessary as taking her next breath. He'd melded in with her brothers as if he'd always belonged.

She looked around at all the people who had gathered for her barbecue, the people she had envisioned when she'd been kept in that shed, and more. There was nothing better than seeing her brothers with their loved ones.

As Tom flipped burgers his gaze went often to his wife, Peyton, and Lilly out in the yard. Caleb sat next to Portia and occasionally rubbed his hand against her bulging pregnant belly. Benjamin had turned in his badge and was now ranching full-time and Edie looked happy to have him at the ranch day in and day out. Finally there was Jacob, who was sitting in a chair next to Layla and smiling indulgently as she talked incessantly without seeming to take a breath.

Over the past year the Grayson family had faced many trials, but they'd all come out stronger, better in the end, and discovered that ultimately the only thing important in life was love.

"I've got the burgers ready," Tom yelled from the grill.

It was like calling cattle to a feed trough. The entire group headed for the table that was already set with salads and condiments, with chips and baked beans.

Brittany wouldn't have thought the cacophony

could grow any louder, but it did as everyone found a seat and the meal commenced.

Alex slid into the chair next to hers and lovingly touched her thigh beneath the table. "How's my woman?"

"Happy," she replied. "Happier than I've ever been in my life."

"That's what I like to hear," he replied, his amazing eyes filled with love.

"I have a little announcement to make," Caleb said. "Portia and I went to the doctor yesterday and it looks like there's going to be another little Grayson boy in the family."

Portia rubbed her big belly with a smile. "And right now we're still fighting over what his name is going to be."

"As far as I'm concerned, this works for now." Caleb leaned over against Portia's belly. "Hey, Boy, how you doing?"

Everyone at the table laughed and the sound wrapped around Brittany's heart. There hadn't been enough laughter in the Grayson family lately but they'd been catching up on that over the past three months.

Brittany had started back to work as a deputy a month earlier, and between that and Alex and Emily, her life was as full as she wanted.

"I also have an announcement to make," Alex said and rose from his seat. "Well, actually, it's not an announcement. It's a question."

Brittany looked at him in surprise as he fell to one

knee at the side of her chair. Her heart fluttered wildly in her chest as she gazed into Alex's eyes.

"Brittany, we've had over three months together," he said as the others fell silent. "Months that have been the best of Emily's and my lives. I want more. We both want more." He pulled a velvet box from his pocket and opened it up in front of her.

The diamond ring caught the sun and sparkled with a brilliance that couldn't compare to the shine in her heart. "Will you marry me, Brittany?"

"Say yes!" Emily said and jumped out of her chair. "Oh, please, say yes and be my mom."

There was never any question in Brittany's mind what her answer was going to be. "Yes," she said. "Yes, I'll marry you."

"Now, that sounds like a plan!" Emily exclaimed with excitement.

Alex pulled Brittany up into his arms, and as they kissed, the family who loved her cheered as if they knew what she did, that the future was bright with love and happiness.

Brittany had survived not only The Professional, but also an imitation of the monster, and that she had survived for one reason—because fate had wanted her here to step into the role of wife and mother. It was her true destiny, she knew as Alex's mouth found hers once again, and she was ready to embrace him and Emily as her very own.

* * * * *

SUSPENSE

Heartstopping stories of intrigue and mystery—
where true love always triumphs.

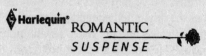

Harlequin® ROMANTIC SUSPENSE

COMING NEXT MONTH
AVAILABLE JANUARY 31, 2012

#1691 HIS DUTY TO PROTECT
Black Jaguar Squadron
Lindsay McKenna

#1692 RANCHER'S PERFECT BABY RESCUE
Perfect, Wyoming
Linda Conrad

#1693 THE PRETENDER
Scandals of Sierra Malone
Kathleen Creighton

#1694 AWOL WITH THE OPERATIVE
Jean Thomas

REQUEST YOUR FREE BOOKS!
2 FREE NOVELS PLUS 2 FREE GIFTS!

ROMANTIC
SUSPENSE

Sparked by Danger, Fueled by Passion.

YES! Please send me 2 FREE Harlequin® Romantic Suspense novels and my 2 FREE gifts (gifts are worth about $10). After receiving them, if I don't wish to receive any more books, I can return the shipping statement marked "cancel." If I don't cancel, I will receive 4 brand-new novels every month and be billed just $4.49 per book in the U.S. or $5.24 per book in Canada. That's a saving of at least 14% off the cover price! It's quite a bargain! Shipping and handling is just 50¢ per book in the U.S. and 75¢ per book in Canada.* I understand that accepting the 2 free books and gifts places me under no obligation to buy anything. I can always return a shipment and cancel at any time. Even if I never buy another book, the two free books and gifts are mine to keep forever.

240/340 HDN FEFR

Name	(PLEASE PRINT)	

Address		Apt. #

City	State/Prov.	Zip/Postal Code

Signature (if under 18, a parent or guardian must sign)

Mail to the **Reader Service**:

IN U.S.A.: P.O. Box 1867, Buffalo, NY 14240-1867
IN CANADA: P.O. Box 609, Fort Erie, Ontario L2A 5X3

Not valid for current subscribers to Harlequin Romantic Suspense books.

Want to try two free books from another line?
Call 1-800-873-8635 or visit www.ReaderService.com.

* Terms and prices subject to change without notice. Prices do not include applicable taxes. Sales tax applicable in N.Y. Canadian residents will be charged applicable taxes. Offer not valid in Quebec. This offer is limited to one order per household. All orders subject to credit approval. Credit or debit balances in a customer's account(s) may be offset by any other outstanding balance owed by or to the customer. Please allow 4 to 6 weeks for delivery. Offer available while quantities last.

Your Privacy—The Reader Service is committed to protecting your privacy. Our Privacy Policy is available online at www.ReaderService.com or upon request from the Reader Service.

We make a portion of our mailing list available to reputable third parties that offer products we believe may interest you. If you prefer that we not exchange your name with third parties, or if you wish to clarify or modify your communication preferences, please visit us at www.ReaderService.com/consumerschoice or write to us at Reader Service Preference Service, P.O. Box 9062, Buffalo, NY 14269. Include your complete name and address.

HRS11B

Discover a touching new trilogy from
USA TODAY bestselling author

Janice Kay Johnson

Between Love and Duty

As the eldest brother of three, Duncan MacLachlan
is used to being in control and maintaining an
emotional distance; as a police captain it's his job.
But when he meets Jane Brooks, Duncan soon finds
his control slipping away. Together, they fight for a
young boy's future, and soon Duncan finds himself
hoping to build a future with Jane.

Available February 2012

From Father to Son
(March 2012)

The Call of Bravery
(April 2012)

*Louisa Morgan loves being around children.
So when she has the opportunity to tutor bedridden Ellie,
she's determined to bring joy back into the motherless
girl's world. Can she also help Ellie's father open his
heart again? Read on for a sneak peek of*

THE COWBOY FATHER

*by Linda Ford,
available February 2012 from Love Inspired Historical.*

Why had Louisa thought she could do this job? A bubble of self-pity whispered she was totally useless, but Louisa ignored it. She wasn't useless. She could help Ellie if the child allowed it.

Emmet walked her out, waiting until they were out of earshot to speak. "I sense you and Ellie are not getting along."

"Ellie has lost her freedom. On top of that, everything is new. Familiar things are gone. Her only defense is to exert what little independence she has left. I believe she will soon tire of it and find there are more enjoyable ways to pass the time."

He looked doubtful. Louisa feared he would tell her not to return. But after several seconds' consideration, he sighed heavily. "You're right about one thing. She's lost everything. She can hardly be blamed for feeling out of sorts."

"She hasn't lost everything, though." Her words were quiet, coming from a place full of certainty that Emmet was more than enough for this child. "She has you."

"She'll always have me. As long as I live." He clenched his fists. "And I fully intend to raise her in such a way that even if something happened to me, she would never feel like I was gone. I'd be in her thoughts and in her actions every day."

Peace filled Louisa. "Exactly what my father did."

Their gazes connected, forged a single thought about fathers and daughters...how each needed the other. How sweet the relationship was.

Louisa tipped her head away first. "I'll see you tomorrow."

Emmet nodded. "Until tomorrow then."

She climbed behind the wheel of their automobile and turned toward home. She admired Emmet's devotion to his child. It reminded her of the love her own father had lavished on Louisa and her sisters. Louisa smiled as fond memories of her father filled her thoughts. Ellie was a fortunate child to know such love.

Louisa understands what both father and daughter are going through. Will her compassion help them heal—and form a new family? Find out in
THE COWBOY FATHER
by Linda Ford, available February 14, 2012.

Love Inspired Books celebrates 15 years of inspirational romance in 2012! February puts the spotlight on Love Inspired Historical, with each book celebrating family and the special place it has in our hearts. Be sure to pick up all four Love Inspired Historical stories, available February 14, wherever books are sold.